Van Boyle

Nathan Leslie

Texture Press

VAN BOYLE
Nathan Leslie

Texture Press
1609 Oklahoma Avenue
Norman, OK 73071

Library of Congress Cataloging-in-Publication Data

Leslie, Nathan, author.
   Van Boyle / Nathan Leslie.
      pages cm
      ISBN 978-1-945784-24-8 (pbk.)

1. Homeless persons—Fiction.
2. Baseball players—Fiction.
3. Fathers and children—Fiction.
4. Maryland—Fiction.
5. Social isolation—Fiction.
6. Memory—Psychological aspects—Fiction.
7. Psychological fiction.

I. Title.
PS3612.E84 V36 2025
813'.6—dc23

Description: Once a major league ballplayer, Van Boyle loses everything after injury, left haunted by the game that defined him and sustained only by the fragile human ties he can still cling to.

Contents

5

At 2:17 a.m. on February 16th Van Boyle succumbed to a prolonged bout of pneumonia. Van fought, always did—wheezing and sweating and shivering. Doctor William Peterson of the regional hospital of Cumberland, Maryland stated that Mr. Boyle struggled against the illness, but that as a result of Mr. Boyle's poor overall physical health, he was unable to shake it off—despite the antibiotics, despite the respirator. His body felt wrung out, spent. Weakness, age. Too many factors aligned themselves against him, the doctor explained. Mr. Boyle lay bedridden in the hospital for seven days prior to his death, having hesitantly checked himself in late Thursday evening, unable to breathe. Unable to move. Paralyzed with fever. Mr. Boyle also suffered from hypothermia as well as severe dehydration, the doctor said. It was too much.

Mr. Boyle's ex-wife, Cheryl Grison, was present at the hospital at the time of Mr. Boyle's death. She loomed over him, clasped his knuckles, ran her forefinger along his temple. She stood there, back straight. She did not weep, but she did embrace him often and her eyes lifted into a faraway trance. She never sat. Not once did she sit.

"Oh, Van," she hushed. "My, my."

At the funeral service Cheryl Grison offered the eulogy. Attendance was scant but it proceeded. Aside from Cheryl, Mr. Boyle's ex-teammate Willie Binker, from Mr. Boyle's baseball days, sat there by himself in a pew of his own. His cousin stood in the corner, almost as if he didn't want to be seen. The attendees believed the multiple winter storm warnings may have kept other potential mourners from showing their respects. It was a frigid, icy day and the sky unleashed intermittent sleet upon the small assembly. The winds bayonetted through even thick clothing.

The pastor did note the sarcastic smile permanently affixed on the deceased visage of Van Boyle. As if he had one more thing to say. As if the joke was on the survivors. During his sermon he detailed the many accomplishments of Mr. Van Boyle, focusing most obviously on his years in Major League Baseball, the high point of his life. Maybe the only high point. The pastor chose not to speak about more recent years to blunt the potential dishonor the family might feel.

Van Boyle's body was not embalmed or prepared, as his will dictated. His coffin was fashioned of unadorned pine. They buried Van Boyle next to his parents in a cemetery in the hills of Central Maryland. His epitaph read "Here rests a fighter." Cheryl Grison propped blue flowers at Van's Headstone. She was seen later—wide rimmed sunglasses masking her eyes—standing under the frozen skeleton of a nearby willow. She remained at the cemetery three hours after the service, holding her umbrella askew into the slanting curtain of sleet.

"I don't want to die," Van hushed in the hospital. "I haven't finished everything."

She held his hand and squeezed once, twice—as a companion, as she used to do. Just like that. She plugged her ears against the wheezing and croaking. She turned her head away towards the blank wall.

68

Van lived in a shabby tent just outside of Accident, Maryland near the Savage River. At this time Van foraged—eating insects, roots, ensnaring squirrels with traps he acquired on the cheap from a farmer from Pennsylvania. His knee ached relentlessly and he hobbled and often resorted to using his cane, but he existed, survived. He subsisted.

Van liked the *feeling* of wisdom, even if he wasn't sure if he *was* actually wise or ever would be. If not at age sixty-eight, when? Maybe at one point, he served the role as a mentor to so many on the fringes—that surely counted for something, didn't it? He watched out for them and they helped him and gave him food if they had some to spare. But in the woods he lived dead alone and frequently hungry. At times the hunger seemed to eat away at his intestines. It gouged him out. Beneath his clothes Van could feel his brittle, spikey bones, his ribs. He didn't dare gaze upon his reflection from the river, petrified what new feebleness he might witness. Once a week he biked to Accident to withdraw money from the shreds of his bank account and to buy staples—bread, rice, cheese, tea, apples. About all he could afford.

For now he had no need for a chair. That was something—an enhancement of sorts, at least temporarily. Once a month or so Van would try to call Joshua and Ashley. A solitary pay phone corroded outside of the town library. Few left. However, when calling Joshua, Van could barely make it past the second ring. He tried. They both knew of this. Occasionally Van would enjoy the privilege of speaking to Ashley, however. She was easier. *If* her husband was not home. *If* she was not in one of her states. And *if* she felt in the mood. Conditions had to align themselves.

"I'm just so glad you're okay. It's so very nice of you to check in, to let us know you are doing well. It's been far too long." She was a person who meant what she said.

Van hoped one day to meet his grandchildren, but Van feared pressing his luck. Too much, too soon and he'd scare off his opportunity—if it still existed. It took him too long to make progress. He harbored regrets.

Van's youth melted into a distant mist. He never knew *this* derelict scouring rested in his future, but now that it was his present his past seemed like *another* person's life, some gauzy dream.

On warm nights Van crouched by the river, dangling his fishing line in the water. Knobby stick on the end. He was not a terrible fisherman—he learned a few tricks over the years. The Savage River consisted of skunk cabbage and fern and moss beds along the shore and Van could rest there. He might snag catfish, carp. A hard spot formed in Van's stomach out there on the river. He felt lonely and his heart desolate and his body knew it. Yet, he felt also cognizant of who he was and where he was and the knot consisted of part shame, part sensitivity, part resolve. He made it that far and that was, in itself, an accomplishment.

Van watched the bobber rise and sink into a dark spot, a veiled eddy. This is me, he thought. What my life has come to.

The Tree

I lived inside a tree for several months and it was the winter and in this patch of woods it was the best shelter I could find. And I didn't see anybody for the entire time I stayed there.

A large tree, looked like lightning struck it at one time, and the edges of the hole blackened and charred.

I felt lucky to find the tree since I had very little money and my car had died, and I needed a place to call my own, to simply breathe.

Most nights I ate canned beef soup or minestrone and that functioned as my meal. That was it. And I foraged for roots in the mornings and found some usually and I lived on them, too.

I left the tree when hunters spotted me, and I could see them slashing through the woods in their orange vests and hats and they took a few shots in my direction and laughed and I packed up then. They smelled of cigars and beer. It was a good place but not worth serious trouble.

My teeth hurt. My eyes hurt. My head hurt. My feet hurt. My legs hurt. My shoulders hurt. My shoulder hurt. I hurt. I hurt.

67

For five hundred dollars Van Boyle agreed to do an autograph session at the Frostburg Best Western. The event celebrated the Baltimore Orioles and the fortieth anniversary of their 1970 World Series Championship. Van did not feel a big part of that particular glory, having just been called up from the farm team, Rochester, in September that year. But he was there. He only had sixteen at bats that year, but plenty of collectors still wanted his autograph on their cards or balls or photos or programs since he was, for a short time, part of the team. A winning team. He too considered himself a champion. The hardcore fans knew his name, some of them—even from such a long time ago.

His teammates gave him high fives and asked how his knee felt, as if the injury just happened yesterday. Van felt appreciative; in a sense the fans looked out for him—for his overall wellbeing. Some players found the fawning masses annoying. But Van felt lucky. His teammates knew his situation, though Van preferred not to talk about it. Jordy and Phil and Dice offered him cash and a place to stay, but Van declined it. It didn't feel *right* to him. Everybody has to take care of themselves, Van knew. Everyone has their own bag of rocks. *They* did take care of themselves; he had to do the same.

Van exchanged glances with Chico, but they refused to speak—not a peep. Van had nothing to say to him anymore, nothing of substance at least. Even the idea of casual pleasantries made him feel nauseous.

The hotel shower and free room helped even more than the cash. Even if it only lasted for just twenty-four hours, he felt like part of *something* again.

Davey lent him a pair of barely worn pants and a red and orange Hawaiian shirt for the occasion, and he bought a razor from the vending machine and used it. The last thing he wanted: for someone he respected to catch a whiff of him or sense his chronic desperation or gather that he struggled overall. That he lacked a home. He refused pity or the attention that would bring.

But gunk lined his fingernails. Nothing he could do about that. A few fans noticed, and one jokingly said, "Looks like you're doing some yard work these days." Jokey smile. They had no idea. They meant no harm.

Van glanced down and said, "All that mulching last weekend—dang garden seems to get better every year." He summoned a smile and he grudgingly nodded and grinned some more, wincing. Pretending? Never a problem for him. He could say whatever, do whatever—it meant nothing to him.

The fans possessed more wealth than he did, tenfold. But did they look out for *him?*

When the event was over, Van tucked the five hundred into his pocket and climbed onto his bike (makeshift duct tape seat) and pedaled back into the woods behind the high school. Every morning he could hear the announcements on the intercom, and when the band practiced he could feel each drumbeat in the hollow depths of his stomach.

But it was winter, and, as a result, a hush settled over his patch of woods. No lawnmowers. No birds. Just breath and chill and attempting to stay warm, whatever it took to make do. He folded the money into his Ziploc bag with his other belongings he kept close. He'd go to the bank soon. He'd have to. The last thing he wanted: some stinking bum making off with his hard-earned bills. Some druggie. Some drunk. He'd buy soup and chicken broth and apples and rice and crackers and more Sterno canisters. He really needed those badly. Basics.

Even though the poplars and beech trees grew thick there and he lived a mile back into them behind some boulders and a rocky outcrop, Van knew the blue would sniff him out soon enough. He always was. He was prepared to pack up and move along though at any time. One day and then the next—the immutable law. He would limp along.

"Homeless"

I'm not homeless. I *have* a home. It might not look like your home, but I have one.

"Homeless" is just a label, a slur as far as I'm concerned.

I make my home where I can. That's what I do.

If anything I'm a wanderer, out of necessity.

Another reason I don't like to associate. I'm my own person, not a member of a group of people.

I'm not homeless. My home is where I make it. I have a home everywhere, or at least I like to think I do. I survive.

14

Social security checks would come, Van knew, *if* he had an address. But that was the requirement. Without an address, the checks would never arrive. Disability checks would be delivered. Without an address though, no luck. He tried to work it out on the phone, but without a phone or an address it was different, nearly impossible.

Van refused to worry though. He'd receive the money eventually, or he wouldn't. In either case, he was alive. A few years back Van never thought he'd see sixty-six. At times he never thought he'd see *fifty*-six. Today seemed like a mirage only years ago, something to offer him false hope.

He built himself a makeshift wheelchair from an old rolling office chair. He duct taped towels and old pillows along the back for a more comfortable fit. The arms of the chair still felt rather flimsy, but solid enough that it could contain him. Van felt ready for what might come. His knee appeared swollen to twice its normal size. The cold days felt especially rough. Some mornings he could barely stand. He *ached*. Shooting pains through his knee, Achilles. He had to hobble.

Van was not even sure exactly where he was—another problem. He knew the location rested somewhere near Oakland, Maryland, but not in it. He found a shipping container in the pines. Nobody out there knew why it rested where it did or how it got there. To Van it was a boon, a sign that the universe protected him, at least for the moment. Better than most situations—it kept him safe and dry.

He could only think of the lake; perhaps some kind of barge floated on it—though it seemed difficult to conceive. Stranger things had happened.

Or perhaps the container was not for shipping at all (his mind showed its age). Perhaps the large steel rectangle was intended as a storage unit and some scofflaw absconded with it, ditched it there in the middle of nowhere.

Van missed Carlos. Without that someone to watch out for him, Van felt like a woebegone child. He needed that person, that someone. Some outsiders might think it irresponsible to become dependent upon someone's assistance, especially when it played such a large role in Van's life. But nothing is childish about camaraderie, about the will to survive, even if it meant relying upon someone more skilled in life. We all must know our limitations, Van knew. Stay within yourself. Know what you are good at, what you struggle with. The failure to do so only asked for trouble.

Each evening Van walked through the pine bowers. He listened to the brush of his feet through the needles, to the meshing of deciduous down the incline. If his knee hurt too much, he used the chair. Sometimes he would use the cane if he felt better.

If Van could find worms or centipedes or salamanders under the rocks and logs he'd take all he could. A Ziploc bag could prove useful. Free protein, and with a little table salt, not unappetizing fried. He looked for ginger root and blackberries during their season. Dandelion leaves were useful, but he needed to find a sunny patch for them. The sun worked wonders. Everything seemed ten times more difficult during the cold weather when he had to resort to canned foods often and he needed more money to make do.

Van had missed out on things—he knew that. However, the trade-off was his version of peace. He would not want his old life back, even if he could have it. Perhaps the security...but otherwise this was the life he seemed suited for, or became suited for. Perhaps he purposefully sabotaged his prior existence out of discontent? Perhaps his desolation could be considered willful? He could not be sure, even himself.

The Time Van Found Something Useful in the Dumpster

I'd seen it all. Dead infants, drugs, guns, baskets and baskets of perfectly good apples (we ate them for weeks), breakup letters, love letters, intimate photographs, jars of pennies, beautiful paintings, and antique masks.

I'd take any and all items of potential value to the pawn shop, if one existed nearby. If not, I'd try to sell it on the corner, or trade it to someone for cigs or food, or something I could actually use.

One time I found a box of 1973 baseball cards—one of two years I actually had a card. I carried some pride in it. I leafed through them anxiously. I lost all my memorabilia in the divorce. So I had no way to prove the reality of my past. And there it was—my card, bent up and frazzled, but still intact; I sold the rest at a pawn shop for five dollars.

I wrapped the card in newspaper and stowed it away in my bag as safe as I could. Some days I'd take it out and look at it: that was me on the big stage. I *did* something with my life. I *was* someone.

There were a few others I kept of my teammates, and I stowed those away, also. It seemed important to remember them, if I could for some reason. Perhaps I was overly sentimental. These long faded images on cardboard.

A few years later it poured down rain, flooding my campsite and my bag became soaked and the cards ruined—as good as soggy toilet paper. Had to toss them—which hurt.

I promised myself I'd find them again someday. I'd like that.

I've Eaten

Just about everything you can imagine. Mr. Williams was right, all those years ago.

I'm not a vegetarian, but I've mostly eaten plants, easier to catch. Don't have to even try. Spring and summer are easy. Dandelions and goosefoot and garlic mustard, chickweed and broad leaf dock. Wild onion. Beech leaves, young green pine shoots, cattail pollen and the sweet inner stalk, clover, field penny cress, fireweed, chicory, laurel cherry, ornamental crab apples and plums. I've made bread from the seeds of dock and it's good.

Of course berries are easy in the later summer—blackberries and raspberries. Acorns aren't bad really. Just have to leach them.

I've eaten amaranth, arrowroot, wild strawberries, sheep sorrel, wild rose.

There's a wealth of weeds I've eaten. They're my go-to.

In the winter it's more difficult to forage when I have to rely on roots and nuts and what squirrels or mice I can conk on the head with my hunting stick—a hard way to go and many calories burnt. I've eaten countless grubs and I've caught many groundhogs and possums and, once, a raccoon.

These are rarities. Snakes are easier to catch and kill—you just step on them, whack them against a trunk and you have a meal, or part of one at least. But only a mouthful—they are small, slender and even smaller cooked.

In the summer it's fairly easy to catch grasshoppers, ants, and caterpillars, plus June bugs, worms and termites if you can find them. Moles and mice are more difficult and usually not worth it. Fish—I prefer fish. Don't even need to cook them.

65

Outside of Martinsburg, Van's buddy Carl owned a 1974 Dodge Caravan with curtains on the windows. It didn't run, but it contained a thin bunk in back and for Van this was enough. It smelled of mildew and warped vinyl seats and must, and the combination of these things made Van cough at night, but it was dry and a place Van could call home, for a while. Behind the defunct Esso station. Feral cats skulked about the van at night, screeching and hissing and moaning at each other. Not a problem. Anything felt better than sleeping in the woods or curled up behind a reeking Dumpster in a desolate parking lot.

"This is the place where we say goodbye," Jenna said. He called her Jenna, though he was sure her real name was nothing close.

Sleet pinged the roof of the van and they ate lima beans and sopped up the juice of it with Wonder Bread.

"What are you *talking* about?"

Van knew she had all kinds of problems, but this was unusual. She *clung* to him. He was a life boat to her, as she admitted in so many words herself.

"You know I don't want to talk about it," she mumbled. They ate and the sleet intensified. The cold shot through his meniscus and he groaned in pain. He rubbed his arthritic knee but it did little to help him. He took aspirin to little effect. Winced.

He had one last candle, and he lit it. Weeks had passed since his last shower, so the candle helped. Maybe. But the stench must have put Jenna off, Van thought. She did not lack odor herself, but he would never utter a word of that. It did not matter.

Still, Jenna usually made for good company and it was helpful to have somebody to speak his thoughts to, if nothing else. He could keep a journal—he had done so before. But this did not feel like a warm comfort, but rather like a duty. A person—that was something.

They sat on the bunk, the candle flickering against the rusted interior walls of the vehicle.

"What's the premonition?" Van thought this might be a worthy approach to addressing the problem.

"I'm lacking one," Jenna said. "I haven't been in one place so long. I may be back."

Van wanted to say that if he could start the vehicle he would. If he possessed the means. *Carl* might, he said. Perhaps we can ramble together, he thought.

"I mean alone," Jenna said. "I'm used to my own habits, not to sharing them."

"You can always go for a walk, or just lean away. There's that."

Van saw all of Jenna's three remaining teeth. She seldom smiled. Jenna rested her head on his flank and eventually Van's heart calmed enough and they slept.

Her satchel remained at the ready when it was still dark. It was a thing, like so many others, he couldn't stop. He couldn't think of a way to at least. She was like a shadow finding itself. Part air and wind. The door creaked and the gust took her off.

The Time a Nice Lady Let Me Borrow Her Credit Card

Her name was Rosalyn McGhee—I'll never forget. For some reason I had a Jonesing for cigs and I was starving and thirsty and out of money and stood at the corner of 3rd and Oak in Frederick, a town I didn't know well. It was sweltering—an evil humidity sopping us all. The sun bounced off the black top and I could barely see and I wished I wore sunglasses.

She walked down third and saw me in the median island, squatting on a cracked milk crate, but she went out of her way, drifted directly to me.

"You look like you could use some relief," she said.

"It's true," I said. She handed me her credit card.

"Just bring it back. I'll wait here for you." I was not expecting this. And I was not a thief.

If I was built differently I could've run off with it, but I went to the gas station on the corner and got my cigs, my sandwich, a bottle of water and I handed it back to her.

"What's your name?"

I told her.

"If I was in your position, you'd do the same," she said.

She kissed my cheek. I will never forget that.

A good day. I slept well that night.

Carl came into enough money for a room, but the landlords acted hawk-eyed and callous. They knew Carl's troubles and made him sign a lease dictating a no-visitor policy as an exchange for the low rent. Carl informed Van of this.

"It's no problem to me," Van said. He still owned the tarp and his bike and his wherewithal.

Carl landed a part-time job collecting tickets at the hot springs, and this was something he told Van. Where nobody would know who he was and where he could slide in for free without any one being the wiser. So Van bathed frequently for a while. Jenna too, by proxy.

It was a good town for scavenging, especially that summer. Plenty of tourists came forth on weekends, and some during the week as well. Pizza and potatoes and French fries and bags of week-old salad and semi-stale cookies filled the Dumpster. A bonanza. Van and Jenna collapsed on a knob near a dilapidated school, where some others slept. Van usually stayed away from hobo villages, but it was the only safe place he could find within shouting distance.

When the sun fell below the mountains, the village would descend into the shadows to reap the rewards from black garbage bags— to hoist each other into Dumpsters, to find the easy pickings. The good stuff.

"I'm exhausted," he told Jenna. "Deep down." They ate stale wheat bread and squash and soft cherry tomatoes retrieved from the large Dumpster behind the Italian restaurant.

"At some point I need to find a place. I'm not sure how much longer I can go."

"You will. We will. Trust in the generosity of the universe," Jenna said. "It often gives freely. To you and to others."

She was sweet and always positive—he knew this. But was it true? A blue light enfolded them—thanks to the tarp and the way the moonlight hit it. Her skin looked taut and dry. She drank freely from a fifth of vodka. Van said nothing.

"I suppose. I'm running out of steam."

"We all do, my man. We all do."

She said this a lot.

He couldn't stop her from drinking. He just wouldn't partake himself, as he knew the detrimental effects. He saw the ravages—the jaundice, the shakes, the walking into traffic, the puking for hours and passing out in it. But this is what she wanted.

It felt hard enough to watch her. She held out the bottle to him.

"Your loss," she said. "You should relax more, be good to your soul."

In the morning they went to visit Carl and he gave them both number 12 for half an hour.

It eased Van's bones.

They soaked in the warm water and luxuriated. Neither had such a nice arrangement in years, they agreed on that.

"Do you want to forget or have you forgotten?"

Jenna watched the bubbles but lifted her head upon receiving the question.

"I *want* to forget. I wish I could have the memories removed. There should be a surgeon for those things."

"There *should* be."

He sighed, in part from exhaustion, in part from the warm water.

"Sometimes I'm not sure what is a memory and what is a dream. I *think* I really remember those days, but it seems different now than it was. So I'm uncertain."

"It was a long time ago." At least she acted nice about it. At least she was kind.

"I've gotten too much sun is probably it. My brain has sizzled from it."

They thanked Carl and walked back up to the knob. To hide from the sun they hunkered under the canopy and played cards, as if waiting for something to happen, as if there was a lifetime ahead of them.

Van distrusted the face cards. Anyone who can't look at me with both eyes, Van thought. Anyone with a sideways glance.

The shade felt good. Let the sun rest for a while, also.

63

Van and Jenna met outside Warehouse C8 in the industrial park. The warehouse hired on Mondays to catch up with the onslaught of shipments. They tasked Van and Jenna and the temps with packing envelopes with erasers and pens and pencils—whatever the order might be. Educational supplies. This seemed ironic to Van, since he lacked an education himself.

It felt hard on the hands. The temps were mostly college kids paying off bills, but the Monday workers consisted of Van and his guys from the trailer park, where they didn't mind men sleeping out under the stars—as long as they stayed over by the drainage ditch. Kept the mosquitoes at bay.

Jenna just found herself booted from her sister's house, though she wouldn't use that phrase herself. The way Jenna told it, her sister thought she became too ornery and wrapped-up in herself. Van guessed it had to do with Scotch, also. Young children lived in the house there. Frederick viewed itself as a family town—at least that's the way Van perceived it.

They worked side by side in the warehouse filling orders. It was hot and dusty and the air poorly ventilated. This was one reason the company couldn't get enough college kids—
the wicked temptation of the ceiling fans rotating way way up there, creating an unfelt breeze. Van felt soaking wet. Though he needed the money to survive, he was glad it was only Mondays. He needed time to recover. He felt too old for this patchwork life anymore.

It had been a long long while since Van slept with a woman. He had forgotten how it felt.

It had been a long while since a woman wanted to put her hands on him.

Van asked if she would go scrounging with him.

"Don't have to, do we? We have enough."

But Van didn't want to waste his money on food, when he hadn't a clue when the next check would come in. I need a roof over my head first, he thought.

But Van bent to her desire, for the sake of the greater good. He wanted her. They splurged for hot cheese and tomato sandwiches and fries at the local greasy spoon.

They found a spot on the loading dock of the middle school. Nobody could see them there unless someone purposefully followed, and they weren't important enough for that. Van knew of the furtive locations, the places where he could burrow away for a night. Out of desperation.

She tasted of barley—her skin, her hair, her mouth. More a tang than a smell. Jenna reminded him, on some level, of vegetable soup. A comfort.

That year he felt inseparable from her. Van found so much warmth and big-heartedness in her. He found so much need. Van wanted to protect her, from herself most of all. She too saw herself cast out, suffering a messy story of divorce and alienation from her own children.

"They were inside me, and now they won't even let me bend their ears. Can you believe that? It's a godforsaken travesty if you ask me."

Jenna was whip-smart and delicate and soon enough people considered them together. The trailer park needed a pure romance or two.

He'd rub her back or give her a hose shower at the facilities. He'd slap the mosquitoes away from her before he'd even notice the ones hovering about *his* head.

24

He liked the way she pressed her feet together as she talked—
heel to toe.

"Let's get married someday," Jenna said. "Build a life together just you and me. We can have a patio and sit out on it at night and peer up at the stars. We can nestle."

Van smiled through the pain—something new to him. His heart slowed to a steady contentment.

"I know it doesn't mean as much now, this late. But still. It's not *too* late, is it?"

Van shook his head and they curled into each other in the shadows. His legs felt like welts, but he didn't care.

The Time Van Thought He Saw Josh in Frostburg, Maryland

I was out there in the cold. It was January and my fingers felt numb, my gloves in tatters. Couldn't even fall under that name.

I made my way to the store and I had ten bucks and I wanted a pack of smokes, and I also wanted some tea and some peanuts if I had enough left over. I was in good shape thanks to the canned goods from the church, but I owned nothing in the way of luxury items. Smokes, tea bags and peanuts: all outside of my range.

It sleeted again and I walked slowly. It sleets here often. Bitter and nasty pings.

About a block ahead I thought I saw Josh walking with a little girl about four years old, maybe five and they held hands. The man had Josh's built, his hair (from what I could see and remember), but I had no idea he *had* a daughter; what an utter shock! My gut dropped.

I picked up my pace and followed them as they passed the store. I tried to find or talk to Josh for so long and I had so many things to say to him.

They walked just a bit faster than I did. I slipped, trying to catch up.

The girl stopped and Josh bent down to help her with her boot. I kept on going, almost there.

But when I stepped right up behind him I could tell: it wasn't Josh. His face looked nothing like my son's.

The sleet slanted down unrelenting and my face stung from it.

"Are you okay?" The man looked concerned.

"I'm sorry," I said. "I thought....your name is not Josh, is it?"

Such a stupid thing to ask.

"No," he said. "It's Dave." I realized at that moment he showed me more kindness than my son would have. I wanted to ask him if he was sure his name was "Dave." Perhaps he was mistaken. But that might seem weird.

He tugged on his daughter's hand and they walked through the sleet and I watched them go. His daughter turned to watch me.

I had so many things to say, but nobody to utter them to. I swallowed them and my gut felt heavy with bile.

62

There was a fish hatchery just west of Sugarloaf Mountain, down a gully past a stand of pines. Van met the owner, Mr. Edgar Fenster, when he carried water from the public bathroom down to his camp under the bridge. Van limped and suffered from a coughing fit and he felt dehydrated and sore and miserable. It was cold and damp and he smoked again, which he knew he shouldn't do but did anyway at times. Fred Slinkton periscoped his neck and asked if he could be of assistance. He set raccoon traps, explaining that they had a habit of making a mess of his business.

"I'm trying to send a message."

"To the coons or me?"

"To them. You, on the other hand, don't look like a threat to my fish that I know of."

Fred explained that he owned the fish farm—tilapia—and that it was just him, since his sons had grown up and earned their MBAs and so forth. They wanted to escape. They wanted the life in town, the fancy restaurants. It was just him.

"What is your situation?"

Van sensed that it was a blameless question, without judgment. However, he felt ashamed about his condition. He must've smelled awful and his clothes must've smelled soiled and they hung in grimy strips about his arms.

"Making do," he said.

"Where are you *staying* is the point?"

Van told him. At this time of the year it was forsaken, a relief, but it still felt exposed and dangerous. He lacked a better place at that moment.

"Why don't you stay by my shed, which must be better? Nobody will bother you and you'd help me out."

"But how would that help you?"

"Human scarecrow of sorts—keep away the vermin and anybody who might have ill thoughts about tilapia, which isn't likely. But still. Something."

It was a symbiotic relationship then, Van thought. Worked for him.

Dreams could be problematic. At night Van could hear the burbling water and the fish thrashing inside. Or he thought he could. Something about it sent his mind whirling into nightmares. In the most jarring of the nightmares his father appeared to him, grinning as he watched Van sleep. The moonlight caught his incisors. When Van lifted his head, his father kicked it, pounding on his forehead with the toe of his boot. His mother watched with a curious expression of annoyance, as if she tried to tell her husband this seemed like bad form. Then he woke up.

In another dream Van ran through the woods in the dark, hunted by dogs. He could hear the large animals in the darkness, gaining ground—panting, barking behind him. Branches and leaves slapped his face. Briars ripped at his skin. But when he turned around his father rode one of the dogs and the smaller dogs followed along behind. Van's father wore cowboy boots and spurs, but he didn't grin, didn't make a sound. His face bore no expression. Van ran through the darkness, shadows and more shadows, terrified until he awoke.

He kept silent about the dreams when he saw Edgar, as he appreciated the safe plot where he could sleep and Edgar brought him bread and cooked potatoes and cans of tomatoes.

One day Edgar asked Van to help him inside the fish hatchery, so Van did. Edgar previously hurt his foot, which limited his movement. Dropped a cinder block on it and it never healed exactly right. He needed help cleaning the tanks.

"My feet aren't so great either," Van said. "Knee actually."

Van refused to ask for money, though he knew he could and he also knew that with Edgar he would most likely find success. He knew this.

In the water the fish swam thick and slimy, undulating in a murky mass just beneath the surface.

"What is your situation? You weren't always sleeping under a bridge, were you?"

"I'm just a guy. It is true I was a ballplayer once," Van said. "But that was a long time ago. I usually don't talk about it. People feel pity for me and I hate that. It's my own doing."

Edgar watched him work on the tanks and he instructed him.

"That's a terrible story, Van. I'm sorry to hear it."

"I was lucky for a few years. Then I wasn't so lucky for many more. And here I am. Still unlucky."

"That's one way to put it."

Van told him things were looking up, however. He said he'd always cultivated optimism, even if some accused him of acting naive. Better innocent than cranky.

"Things will get better for me, I can feel it."

"I hope it's true."

Edgar told Van that he went into fish farming as a way to make a little money on the side—he worked as a paralegal for years. But then he lost interest in the main job, retired, and invested everything in fish. So far, so good, he said. "My wife is happy I'm around more. So am I. I see myself in a different light. It's a different life than I expected, that's for sure. This is not what I imagined for myself."

But the dreams didn't abate. Van tried sleeping in different corners of the property, but nothing helped. He began to believe the land was truly cursed and that he must leave.

It was looking a gift horse in the mouth, part of him thought. But the other part of him was exhausted from waking up frightened and out of sorts.

One morning he left. He packed his things and headed off on his bicycle. He possessed a clean mind, but he knew on some level he could also be making a mistake. Leave on a high point, but could it go higher? But nothing like a bad dream. He shook his head and kept going.

Showering

Was difficult, always. If I could find a park (with free entrance) I'd use that. Hard to come by and it was usually it was a river, a lake, a fountain, though most were public. If it rained a great deal and the temps were warm I'd strip down and I almost always had a towel stashed away for the occasion.

Most commonly I'd find a gas station, a Hardees, a Pancake House. There I could do face, chest, underarms, hair, back of the neck. A Polish shower. A Mexican shower. A Racer's shower. Went by different names. I hated smelling of shit or baked-in funk.

Someone would often interrupt, stare me down, kick me out.

In warmer weather I'd wander neighborhoods, sneak back to a garden hose or spigot and if nobody watched this would work in a pinch.

29

I hated smelling myself, my filth. I grew up clean and prideful. Nobody likes to smell unpleasant or offensive. Even us. Sometimes we just do as a result of circumstances. We have to smell of feces and body odor and dust and dirt. I tried not to.

61

I'm ten times smarter than even seven years ago, Van thought. And he *knew* it was true. He knew that even though he possessed very little money and no house at all he would be fine. He knew he would *endure*. He would subsist. It's all about being smart, he thought. Picking and choosing.

Van learned to stay away from the city where he felt far too exposed, too vulnerable to crimes and misdemeanors, at the mercy of others like him, many of whom have a litany of problems far more serious and nettlesome than his. Too many people—chances are something would go wrong there. Van learned to avoid crowds altogether and stick to the countryside, to the thickets and copses and small towns near and around them. Even towns could be a risk, really. You just didn't know what might happen if people hung about. He knew he'd be better off alone, isolated, as long as he could handle the loneliness.

And he could.

Van had been alone all of his life, even when married, even as a husband and father. He was alone. Distracted. In his own world. Separated from everyone else somehow. Cheryl frequently said it was as if he left the car running on the curb, waiting for something else to happen. His mind drifted away elsewhere. He couldn't sit still. He fidgeted. He jittered. He felt alone as a child, always—literally or otherwise.

Another year in the ditch. Van found the perfect spot—a gulley above the train tunnel, nestled in the woods, hidden from view. It was protected from the wind and weather and was warmer as a result. The ditch sat in an area where nobody would care if he slept out under the

30

stars. For weeks at a time Van would not see a single soul. A river ran close by, also—which helped.

Occasionally a couple out on a hike. Occasionally a hobo looking for a nook. Usually nobody.

The unspoken rule was first come, first served. He protected his, knife in hand if he had to.

Van's knee ached and he resorted to aspirin he bought with what money left in the account. It never seemed to help much, only dulled the pain. But a dull pain was better than a sharp pain. A sharp pain meant perhaps the hospital.

The downside of the ditch was its location—nowhere close to a grocery store. The nearest store lay four miles back on Route 40, so Van had to think things through, squirrel away the remains. Forage and hope for crayfish and insects to fill the void in a pinch. And then bike or find help, scare up food when he could.

His teeth hurt.

When he biked to the grocery store he'd try Joshua and Ashley, normally without success. It had been years since he spoke to Josh. Ashley would listen to him ramble if he got lucky enough to get her on. If her husband, Joe, answered Van would simply hang up.

So many things to tell them and no way to do so. He thought about sending them letters again, but he imagined that they most likely tossed the envelopes in the garbage upon receipt. What was the point?

Then came Elly. He had no idea how she found him, but when he woke up one bitterly cold March morning there she was, standing in front of him in her corduroy pants and green and yellow plaid shirt.

"It's been some time, no?"

She was European. He forgot from which country exactly. Hungary? Romania? The Czech Republic.

"You skipped out on us, man," she said.

"What are you talking about?" Van said. "I don't exactly have an obligation in the world. If I did I wouldn't be out here, would I?"

31

He could play the question game, also.

"We were part of something, and you wanted to escape. Just be truthful. I'm not some wide-eyed protégé."

It might as well have been another life, as far as Van was concerned. He wasn't hung up—she was. He didn't want any stupid fucking cult membership. If he did, he would seek that out. He wanted to be left alone to his own ruminations. He wanted to find his family, find a way to feel better about himself somehow, die in peace under warm blankets.

He zipped the tent flap closed, but Elly kept yammering.

He knew he simply must leave the ditch, as much as he loathed to do so. Otherwise, he would never hear the end of it.

"Look, I'm still *sleeping*," he said. "You understand that?"

Elly smacked her hand on the side of the tent and wouldn't back down. So Van pulled out. He stood up and showed his teeth—he knew how to do that. Perhaps deep-rooted simian behavior he remembered from school. Subconscious and conscious simultaneously.

"Get. Away. From me," Van said. He said it slowly and calmly so she wouldn't run off to the police. That was the last thing he needed.

She backed away, a rustle in the leaves.

"I'm coming back," she said. "You can't just *leave* people like that."

He watched her back.

That morning he packed up and hit the road. Too bad because he was just getting the hang of it.

60

There was Elly. There was the Colonel and Ron and Bob and Amber and Pancho. They lived in the yellow ramshackle house in the hills. Smelled of mildew. Roof dripped. Vultures swooped up into the rafters and at night, owls. Eventually they affixed duct tape and clear plastic bags up on the window frames to at least keep the birds away.

Van lived there for many months, and this woman Elly was in charge. She was short and skinny and pale. Van thought of her as a tomboy, except she wasn't a boy. Perhaps a *mannish* woman, with a quick wit and a fast temper. She called herself "homely."

They made do Elly's way—scraping and saving everything and working odd jobs. Plus, Elly stole. She didn't advertise it as such, but she stole. Van knew but chose not to confront her about it, or think about it. He didn't want to cause a problem. As long as it was small things.

Elly got on Van's last nerve and he knew she knew it. He likely got on her nerves, also.

The colonel was fine—an ex-vet who suffered terribly from the shakes and struggled sleeping at night and self-medicated with Old Turkey and whimpered about gunfire and tunnels and leeches and whores. But he was a kind man underneath the problems.

Brothers Ron and Bob—everybody called them "the twins," but they weren't twins. Ron was a year older. They *did* look alike—tall and rangy and pointy shoulders and pock-marked cheeks. They were quiet men, and murmuring to each other was their primary means of communication. Amber made do selling her body and she was usually the only one in the house who had any money worth speaking about. She chewed gum relentlessly, saying that it kept the constant clammy taste in her mouth at bay. Van liked to tell her that she might chew right *through* her teeth one day. Pancho didn't speak a lick of Spanish, despite his nickname. Everyone just called him Pancho for some unknown reason— some insider joke that dissipated into an afterthought a long time ago. He felt lethargic and angry and sat around barking at the twins in his throaty rasp and asking Amber if he could borrow twenty bucks.

Van felt far from happy living with this group, but he did so anyway. He wasn't sure why—once he got used to them he found that he had a difficult time motivating himself to leave.

A mile away a sizable cave sat tucked back behind the oaks and sumacs and poplar in a rocky nook of the hills. Van would escape Elly's house from time to time—bike back to the cave. He could find peace back there. He could think clearly. Occasionally he'd sleep in the cave but Elly would reprimand him upon his return, so he rarely stayed long.

People are worth avoiding, he thought. That's an almost universal law.

When Elly came back wearing a gold necklace one day, Van seized on the opportunity. He didn't ask her about it or accuse her. He balked at saying a word to anybody else. He just vanished—poof—early one winter morning with the hope that he'd never see her again in his life.

The Boat

There are many boat bums. You just don't see them unless you're in the water or skulking around the docks.

At one point I lived on a boat in the Chesapeake. I found a small island—a glorified sand-bar, more or less, and I anchored near it, using the island as my privet and a place I could go to find my legs.

Food was tough to come by, so was potable water but I fished all day and ate whatever I caught—crabs, crappie, catfish, eels. I needed to sail to the mainland for water frequently and, I'm not going to lie, it was a pain. There was a pier with a hose, I remember that, but from time to time the water silted-up. A number of five gallon jugs rattled around on the vessel and the water all tasted heavily of plastic, but better than nothing.

Unfortunately I was not a skilled sailor and often I went in the wrong direction or around and around in circles. I had a difficult time backtracking and sometimes I resorted to sleeping out on the open bay. I didn't like this. I wanted to be close to land and I feared the thought of being swept away to sea.

On a trip back to the mainland for water and bananas and bread my vessel began filling with water and I tried to bail it out, but it was of no use. I just left it there at the pier, sinking into the murk and I felt lucky to make it back to solid land in time. Two feet under me, grateful to be walking.

59

It wasn't the city proper, but it was *urban*. People walked and stood and sat everywhere...

He had shingles and needed care.

He had several abscesses that needed attention. Bladder problems. He needed to comfort his body, or else. The pain was too much.

After the hospital he went to live in the United Methodist basement. They had a charity shelter and food and beds. He felt tired and he thought too much about Cheryl and the kids and they *had* to be wondering where he was and what he was doing and was he okay. It tore him up.

He was okay, or told himself to be.

He lived with Leaf and Big Bill and Shoeshine Annie and Krazy Karen and a Russian everyone called the Tzar and A.K. and Sunshine and Movie Mike and Magazine Mike and Meth Mike and Kissing Kevin and Old Man Henry and Basketball Bill and Rainy Day Sam and Money Mike. Everybody possessed a nickname and nobody was who they said they were. And, as a result, few could be clearly trusted.

It was a lot of people to deal with. They called Van "The Philosopher." He had "experience," many said. He knew what "was going on" he spent some time thinking things through. Doesn't everybody? Van wondered. But they didn't. Some people seemed all surface, he learned long ago. Some people would stab you in the head and steal everything you had just to give them a small leg up. It took him years to realize that.

It was lights-out at ten, but even after that A.K. and the Tzar would play seven card stud under the pale red glow from the Exit sign. They bet hundreds of thousands of non-existent money. "I'd clean up if we were playing with real dough," the Tzar said. "It was the best fun in town."

"If we were playing with real money," A.K. said, "I'd play smarter, different somehow. I wouldn't rush it. Know what I mean?"

"Sure you would," the Tzar said. He smiled, knowing.

"I would, and that's a damn fact."

Big Bill ate ferociously—as much as he possibly could. He ate as if his food insulted his mother. As if he was *killing* the food by eating it. As if he wanted to destroy every particle of food he could.

Shoeshine Annie shined shoes for a living. She said it kept her humble. She said she felt lucky to have anything at all. She must've been beautiful in her youth.

Krazy Karen wasn't crazy, just eccentric. She wore Christmas sweaters all year round and called herself a "face painter." Almost nobody at United Methodist would let her near their face. But she said she painted "up here" (pointing to her head). She said she painted in her dreams.

There were lots of Mikes. Magazine Mike made money on the side selling magazine subscriptions from pull-out cards. He charged $1 per subscription. Movie Mike could quote entire passages from classic movies. Verbatim. Money Mike kept a wad of cash taped to his leg—that way nobody would steal it.

They mostly got along.

Sunshine seemed cheery and bounced rather than walked.

Leaf was a nature lover and smelled of manure and humus and dried leaves and muddy creek beds.

Old Man Henry could not afford the retirement center and he didn't have family. He was eighty-six. Rainy Day Sam was only alert when it rained. He loved a rainy day. His migraines, he said, they drove him bonkers. They shot through his skull like lightning. His temples pounded in pain.

Basketball Bill played with anyone and everyone out in the public courts a block from the church. He didn't care at all. He'd shoot baskets until he could barely walk. He'd shoot baskets until his arms fell off.

Everyone had their means of coping.

Van felt ready for something else. He felt hoary and brittle and hemmed-in, forced to speak. He heard an old house still stood up in the hills. That sounded promising.

57

Van loved Maryland. Having been all over the country playing ball, he knew. There was something about it—the proximity to water, the smallness, the green. The hills—he loved the hills the most. Something about them. It was a place in the middle of things and easy to deal with somehow.

Van felt glad he did not own a car any longer. Who needed the hassle? The vehicle made his life cage-like, oppressive. Without it he could experience the world again. And he loved the open sky. Van wanted to stretch his eyes and live again and he felt optimistic he would.

Ashley was right, he needed to think about connections—about the people he knew who might like to help him. He seemed down on his luck, but not out of it completely. He still had something to offer. He was good with his hands. He was competent, valued in his own way.

So when he called Shep, Van felt in a positive mindset. He felt cheerful about the future, despite it all.

"Hey, yeah. Van. Wow, good to hear from you," Shep said. Van explained his state of affairs and Shep told him he was always welcome. He was family and family stuck together no matter what.

"Look at me—I'm spouting clichés," he said. "But I mean it. It comes from the heart, man."

So Van moved in. Shep owned a three bedroom split-level near Oxford, Maryland. It was flat and hot and the small yard was swampy and mosquito infested, but Van showed his appreciation. He promised to do little things around the house to help out, even if nobody asked him to. "A permanent Mr. Fixit, at your disposal." He made good on this right away with some drywall repairs, painting the downstairs bathroom, power washing the deck. They both were estranged from their mutual fathers. Both divorced. They had much in common.

Shep drank heavily though. He drank beer and hoarded the cans and vodka bottles and whisky bottles and the house smelled of booze and piss—sour and bitter. Van struggled with it and he slept with a blanket over his nose, stink-eying shelves of empty vodka bottles.

But Shep didn't mind if Van smoked inside, so Van did—with what little money he had left. Cheryl still sent him occasional pity money, which he hated but accepted. It was often all that filled his paltry bank account.

Shep went off to work at the Crab Shack and drank more there. Van stayed at home and watched old movies or played solitaire when Shep worked. He tried to ignore the bottles by imagining them as receptacles for ketchup. It was not easy.

One night the phone wouldn't stop ringing. Van usually ignored the phone entirely, but after the fourth call he picked it up. The police. Shep had hit a pedestrian, drunk driving. The pedestrian was in critical condition—brain injury. Van needed to help.

He was able to contact Shep's ex-wife, Brandi, who (hesitantly) posted bail. But it didn't matter: Shep was going to jail—clear as day. Brandi decided to rent out Shep's house. He would need the income. Van seemed, as a result, the odd man out. Brandi acted apologetic, but she also made the observation that bad luck seemed to follow him. He's just that kind of guy.

"Probably true," Van said. "How did you know?"

"Word gets out," Brandi said. "It's not a mystery to me. I can see it written all over your face."

Brandi asked if Van had any interest in Van's can and bottle collection. "All yours. Resell it, I don't care."

"No," Van said. "I apologize. I can't help you there."

"Well, you don't have a car," she said. "It makes sense."

She took them all to the recycling center.

"Screw it, she said. "Bad omen." She just wanted them all *gone*.

"Good luck with the house," Van said. "And everything else. I wish you the best."

"You'll be okay though, right? I do feel bad."

They stood in back, in the weeds. Sound of crickets, cicadas. Felt good to be outside.

"I'll be fine."

The Time Van Went for a Walk at 3:07 a.m.

It's not that easy to fall asleep, even in a station wagon. Actually, falling asleep was easier than *staying* asleep. I'd fall asleep when darkness descended but I always woke up to the distractions of near silence: the buzzing of the street light, the clicking of an air conditioner.

One winter evening I woke up and I simply could not go back to sleep. I parked near the elementary school under some trees and it had snowed and the branches sagged under the weight and it felt cold. I wrapped myself as tight as could be in four blankets. When I was a baby I remember my mother driving me around and around to lull me to sleep—always Mom. But I can't drive *myself* to sleep. That was an impossibility.

I decided to walk to the Rite Aid about a mile away since I wanted a carton of milk, which would help me go back to sleep. Milk does. I also wanted to tire myself out, and walking through the snow would do the trick.

So I did—I walked there and bought a carton of milk and drank it and walked back and my feet felt frozen from the snow, but the neighborhood was utterly silent. Porch lights and snow and reflections of the lights on the snow. Most notably silence. I marvel at silence in the middle of the night when I could do anything and nobody in the world would know. It was a beautiful kind of freedom.

As approached my car I saw a red fox crossing the street. He stopped there and stared at me and I stopped and stared and him. We gauged each other for about five minutes, seeing who would make the first move and I must've shuffled my foot forward or made some kind of imperceptibly small movement because the fox bolted into the woods and vanished on his own errand. I thought, just for a moment, of Kat.

I crawled back into the trunk and draped myself with every blanket I owned and I fell right back to sleep then.

The Time Van Hissed At a Woman

Just because I'm on a street corner with a sign around my neck doesn't mean I necessarily want to talk. I stood in Georgetown, trying to scare up some lunch: Washington, D.C., Richie rich. My strategy: stay for two hours, see what I could get from the tourists, leave before I became a *fixture* and I wanted them to *see* me and let the pity and pathos dig down into them. That's how it works.

This lady approaches me, wants to tell me her life story and she says it looks like I could use some cheering up.

"I've heard it all," I said. I wasn't in the mood, I suppose. Tired. Hungry. Bored.

She tells me she's a librarian and that she felt great compassion for the mentally ill. Her sister was schizophrenic, she said—a real shame. She asked if I knew her sister. What do I know every single mentally ill lady?

Then she tells me she wants to take me in, to help me, to save me from myself.

"I don't need that," I say. I couldn't listen to her all the time because she just wanted to run her mouth at me so I turned away, but she kept going.

Then I stuck out my fuming teeth at her and hissed as loud as I could, like an iguana, a python, like a deranged cat. I even terrified myself.

She stepped back, and I walked down to the other corner.

I did not hear her follow me, but she looked over at me several times, as if I would harm her—which I would never do.

That was the point.

56

Van felt creaky. When he awoke, *everything* hurt. He could barely walk as a result of his knee, and his right shoulder ached—his Achilles tendons felt so frail it seemed they were formed of ice. His neck felt stiff from sleeping in the back of the station wagon, his eyes blurred, his stomach roiled with sourness. He had little choice.

Van's bank account was completely depleted and he also lacked steady employment. He could search but he didn't have the energy. Malnourished. Anemic. He hardly had enough money for gas. Van's old credit cards still sat in his wallet, but they were all but worthless now— frozen as a result of nonexistent payment. If he had an address he might be arrested on the spot, for all he knew.

Van slept in the station wagon on the shoulder of an out-of-the-way road by the swimming pool. Occasionally somebody would drive by.

Van's ex-wife's house (his ex-house) rested a mile or less down the road. It bothered him to no end.

"Fuck this shit," Van said.

He drove over to the old house and parked on the street opposite, and he slept there for several hours. He watched the house, as if it might get up and run away. Nobody was home.

A rap on the trunk window woke him.

"Hey." Timothy. Great. "What the hell are you doing here?"

Van pointed to the house. "Cheryl has something for me, I think," Van said. He immediately regretted the "I think," as it showed a sign of ambiguity, a lack of bearing.

"Yeah? What does she have?"

Van shrugged. "You know *her*. It could be anything."

That worked—Timothy showed a twinkle of recognition. He too *knew* Cheryl.

"Hold on. She'll be home soon," Timothy said, and strutted off, chest jutting out.

When Cheryl pulled into the driveway in her gleaming, green Lexus, Van just watched her. The Lexus was the color of a jungle insect. He rolled the windows down. She didn't see him, but he watched her open the trunk of her car and withdraw several Macy's bags from it.

"I'm in trouble with Tiny Tim," Van said.

"Oh, jeez," Cheryl said, surprised. "What are you *doing* here? You know this is not okay."

"I don't know. I was just driving around and I felt tired all of a sudden. Low blood sugar, I think."

"You pulled this with Ashley, too. What's this, some kind of reunion tour?"

They talked. Cheryl said it wouldn't be a great idea—that he needed to leave ASAP. He needed to go home.

"I *am* home," he said, rapping his knuckles on the dashboard.

Cheryl looked him over, her eyes wistful and swollen.

"One night," she said. "I'll talk to him."

"I don't need to stay here," Van said. "I'm just reminding myself of what I am missing out on. I know I blew it. I just wanted a gentle reminder for my own growth."

She looked him over.

"I've been everywhere, all over the place."

"Don't be an ass," Cheryl said. "Come in and get some food and rest for now."

So Van did. Cheryl brought him a bowl of Spanish rice and beans and two chicken thighs. She had Van in the basement, with the crickets. The crickets reminded Van of his new reality. He felt like a prisoner.

"Thank you," he said, and he ate. He slept well in his old house. His body seemed to even ease into it again. He remembered painting that

42

guest room with Cheryl. They listened to old blues records while they worked.

In the morning, a knock on the door.

"Let's go, old timer," Tim said. "Cheryl's gone to work. Time to get on out of here now."

What were Van's options? Other than physical violence, few and far between.

If only he could find a way to *convince* Tim. He was a better man. Couldn't Tim see that?

He lacked the confidence, the moxie. He lacked the words to do the job.

It's just *instinct*, he thought. Better than drowning in the ocean in the prime of his life.

55

Van never liked traveling, even in the majors—always a hassle and it took him away from home, where he wanted to be. That's all he ever wanted—a home and to be in it. But Van also wanted his daughter in his life, but since she lived in Arizona that's where he needed to go.

As he drove, Van remembered those long bus rides in the minors. It was all he could do to stay awake, and sometimes he let himself slip under.

He was not particularly interested in the scenery then; he spent most of his time staring at the back of the thick plastic seat cover in front of him. Van just wanted to *be* there, playing ball—not on his long way *getting* there. Now in his 50's Van felt more attuned to the world outside. He watched the trees turn to mountains to trees to fields of corn and soybeans to fields of barley and wheat. He noticed a symmetry. A progression. The flatlands calmed him. He felt he would return to the earth, that it would accept his skin and bones.

When he arrived in Arizona he called, but after twelve rings no answer. Not a problem. He knew her address and he also knew she was probably in class and that she'd be back. It was April—where else would she be? Van found her street; he found her apartment building. He parked outside of it and waited.

Been some time. Van worried that he would not recognize her.

He made sure he didn't fall asleep, though his drive exhausted him.

He saw her pull into the lot and stand out of her car—taller now, hair curlier, arms tanned and ringed in bangles and plastic bracelets. She wore an orange sun dress and sunglasses. Van stepped out of the car and followed her. She walked up two flights and Van watched her unlock the door to 3B and enter it.

He waited in the stairwell for a long time. If only he possessed the courage.

This is not the way in which he wanted to see his only daughter. His hair felt and looked greasy and unwashed and he smelled of B.O. and must and peanut butter and smoke. He had very little to offer.

But if not at that moment, when?

He was there. She breathed only a few feet away.

He walked up the stairs, hands shaking. He rapped lightly on the door. He heard footsteps and the door opened.

"Oh, my God," she said. "Oh my God."

"Hi, Ashley."

She looked away, down the hall past him. She exhaled.

"I just want to see you. It's been a long time."

She didn't cry; he knew she could be tough.

She just stood there, arms crossed, shaking her head. Her face clenched into a boil. She didn't say anything for a long time.

"I'm sorry. I can't do this." She shook her head a long time.

She shut the door slowly, holding up her hand. As if to say "I'm sorry." As if to say, "Talk to you later." As if to say, peace. As if to say, stop.

He couldn't knock again. He didn't want a problem. Everything would be fine, he told himself. It's fine. I'll try again, later, when she's ready. If.

54

Things crumbled down around him; he could feel it. His family, his marriage, everything he constructed slipped into the steady process of erosion. And it happened quickly, a mudslide.

Van never planned on becoming close to The Handler. It wasn't a *personal* relationship. Maybe it should have been—maybe it would have worked better that way. If the Handler *knew* him, maybe he wouldn't have done what he did. The Handler was his money guy, the one who took care of his bank account, his investments, his finances. A small man— with a small voice and a little pin head. His hair was black and often greased back and he wore dark pants and a white shirt on an almost daily basis—his personal uniform. His eyes dashed and scurried about. He nodded too easily.

But after Silver, Van needed a place to crash. He couldn't afford a place of his own any longer. He needed to lay low, also. Since it didn't work out with the girl—or any girls—he just wanted to fade into the background for a bit, let everything else slide.

The Handler handled others, too. But he liked to be modest. Though the Handler most likely made as much as his famous clients all said and done, he still lived in the same two bedroom condo by the lake. He liked it there. He said it calmed him and that's what he needed— calming. Van knew it must be stressful to deal with all those investments, to be responsible for so much. Pressure cooker.

The Handler felt no desire that Van stay with him, Van could tell that much. He didn't have to say a word. But Van said it's either that or I'll have to let you go, so the Handler acquiesced. Was it *resentment* that drove The Handler?

"It's fine, VB," The Handler said. "It's only temporary. It's good."

He thought of Kat from time to time. He hoped she was at least safe—bare minimum.

Van felt suspicious for several years. He knew his account seemed thinner than it should, but this was just an intuition. By nature Van was generous. He suspected, but not on a deep level—just a passing thought. Mostly he trusted The Handler. He shouldn't have.

When The Handler was out, Van poked around. The Handler was good at hiding his tracks. The paperwork seemed legit—statements, receipts—and it illuminated little deception. But Van felt something amiss; he kept digging.

Then Van found the red folder. Inside the red folder: statements from The Handler's accounts—not Van's. Van looked closely. He saw the numbers, but then he saw the description—transfer from account 00198 to account 12579—from Van's to The Handler's. There were a number of such small transfers—a thousand every month or so. That was it. That was exactly it. The air slowly seeping from the balloon—his balloon.

Not only had The Handler been making poor investments, offering unfortunate guidance, but he also was into some serious skimming. Van felt foolish to have missed the signs. This was the evidence.

But what to *do* about it? Van could easily take the statements to a lawyer and sue The Handler for everything he had. He could inflict physical pain upon The Handler, catch him by surprise when he returned. Van could find a way to steal back from the thief. The Handler acted like a weasel and Van possessed a strong sense of justice.

If The Handler lived in a detached house he'd burn it to the ground. He'd *enjoy* that. But he didn't and Van could not be culpable for the innocent above and below.

As the hours passed, Van grew less and less angry. This was not the plan. For some reason he had a difficult time feeding the fire. I don't

46

know, Van eventually thought—he has to live with himself. He's an even lonelier man than me, Van thought. The Handler could sit for hours staring off into space.

So he's out of my life, Van thought. He packed up his things and left. He'll never hear from me again, Van knew. And vice versa. Van called his bank and changed his account and access. When Van closed his eyes he could see the Handler burning. He'd burn for eternity, Van thought. *That* he could never escape. But beyond that what could he do?

53

She was twenty-one, but an old twenty-one. Wise beyond her years, Van thought. He knew this was a cliché but he could not help thinking it anyway. Her name was Kat and as far as Van could tell, she seemed flawless.

Van met Kat when she was still in school. She was the daughter of the couple who lived next to him at The Terrace. He scarcely spoke to her then, but when he saw her at the grocery store, should at least say hello, should he? Common courtesy, wasn't it?

They stood in the breakfast aisle—boxes of cereal and jam and tea. She dropped two boxes of sugary cereal in her cart and Van smiled at her and watched her, just for a few seconds.

"You used to live next door to my parents," she said matter-of-factly.

"Did I?" Van didn't want trouble.

"You remember me," she said. "Come on now."

They chatted for fifteen minutes right there in the cereal aisle. Kat wore heavy mascara—thicker than he would like—the kind favored by her generation. She possessed an interesting face. She was not classically beautiful. But the way she pursed her sexy mouth. The way she tilted her head. The gleam of light on her neck. She often bore an ironic expression on her face, as if she waited for something to happen. It was something else to see her there, matured, just graduated, filled with positivity. She told Van of her many professors, of the ones she admired. "It's the personalities that stick with me most of all," she said. "I just enjoyed the aura." Van could tell. She handed him her card—she walked dogs during the summer. If he owned a dog to be walked she wanted him to give her a call. Her lips. The way she swayed, as if she had all the time in the world. She did not—neither one of them did.

When Van entered her it was with considerable trepidation, but that trepidation made the ecstasy that much more intense. He felt terrified. He felt immediately guilty, even though Kat assured him, rubbing his arm—there was nothing to feel guilty *about*. They are just following natural animal instincts. The fact that he could easily be at least her father was just a numbers game to her. What matters is the soul, she said—the connection between two people. Kat had a way of easing him, making him feel like a part of something larger than himself. He thought of her as deeply *spiritual* at a deep, universal level. But was it right? He hadn't a clue.

She asked him to move in, with the caveat that her parents still helped her with her bills. They could drop in, but usually they would call first, she said. He felt too far gone to say no.

As far as Van was concerned, they lived in bliss. She hurried off to work and Van helped out around the apartment, cleaning and going to the grocery store and doing little small errands to help her. He felt like a kept man for the first time in his life. How different this seemed to his marriage, where he felt as if he constantly bore the burden of responsibility. With Kat he felt free and spirited and at ease and relaxed. He never thought of it as an illusion. He felt he was stealing one from the world.

Then the worst did happen after all. Her parents were already in the apartment when he returned with the dry cleaning one morning. Kat had given them a key—they paid for most of her rent, after all.

They eyed him as if he were a two-headed cannibal.

"What are *you* doing here?" Mrs. Stitter said.

Van stood his ground, as if he knew this moment was inevitable all along.

"Your daughter…is letting me stay here," he said. "That's all."

"Oh, Jesus Christ," Mr. Stitter said. "You've got to be kidding."

He couldn't help defend himself when Mr. Stitter came at him. He couldn't help himself; he insisted nothing was wrong.

"She *is* an adult," Van said. "Don't worry your head over it."

"An adult," Mrs. Stitter said. "Don't give me that. Yeah, that's what she is. She can't even manage a checking account. *Adult*, please."

"She's strong."

"Let me tell you something—you are an evil predator."

He never saw the punch coming, only felt it reverberate through his jaw.

Kat insisted that he stay, and said it was her problem, not his. But this seemed too much of a burden on him. The calm ruptured.

With Van it always did.

He knew he might never see Kat again. Though he constantly saw her behind his eyes, when he closed them. He could smell her in the middle of the night. He heard her voice underneath his ear. It reverberated, a kind of haunting.

Luckily he did own one single photo of her and he kept it with him in his wallet, folded, in a plastic sheath. For protection.

52

Van admired the hell out of Eddie "Silver" Gunn—and that was part of the problem. Van was known and respected; Eddie was a star among stars. He struggled with injuries and it ruined him, it took him out. Eddie acted so smoothly. Everything came easy to him. Eddie owned the big house, the fat wallet, women at his disposal. Eddie was pampered.

Van fought and scrapped for everything he got, and even then it wasn't as much as he wanted, as he felt he *deserved*.

Once he was evicted from the apartment, Eddie invited Van over. "Man, mi casa is su casa," he said. Eat what you want. Drink whatever, man. Sleep wherever. Live it up. You have only one life, that's the way I see it."

Eddie had invested wisely. His money went to bonds, some stocks, savings. Eddie went to the University of Massachusetts. He knew what was what, even after fifteen years in the big leagues. Van admired that, also. There was a reason Eddie was Van's best friend in baseball and they were roommates—though those days seemed two lifetimes ago.

Van never understood why Eddie was friends with *him*. What did Eddie get out of the situation? To Van, it seemed unbalanced.

Van slept in Eddie's daughter's room, painted pale green with yellow trim. "She was a nature girl, still is," Eddie said. She was off to college, living on her own. Her bed felt firm and restful. The room smelled faintly of rosewater and perfume, or perhaps this was just his imagination. Van hadn't slept so well for years.

Van had a blast with Eddie that summer. Like old times. They went out to eat, golfed, trips to the beach—all on Eddie's dime. On top of everything, Eddie was so *generous*. It was too much, really.

"I don't mind," Eddie said. "I'm alone a lot."

His wife insisted upon working a day job, though they didn't need the money. Eddie said she wanted to feel responsible. "We're happy," Eddie admitted. Van had never seen a couple so at peace, so content. They made good choices. Van did not.

When the three of them went out to dinner (which was frequently) Van watched the eyes. He could see that other women viewed Eddie as attractive. Their bodies shifted when he walked into the room. A shame, a turn of the wrist, a finger to the hair. He was a magnet for admiration.

Eddie's daughter's room seemed larger than his entire efficiency. They had a cook for breakfast and dinner. Van ate eggs Benedict three times a week. His toilet paper culminated in triangles and hand towels pinched into delicate shapes.

This is an oasis, Van told himself. Enjoy it while you have it because it won't last for long. For a while Van lavished—he took it all in. Everything had been so *hard* and he knew it would be even more difficult later. He was fifty-two years old. His life was well more than halfway over. If he was lucky he'd have another thirty years, though nobody ever knows. And some of those would be of low quality. Sixty more dental appointments in his life if he went every six months and lived thirty more years. Thirty more appointments if he lived to sixty- seven. That's not that many. Dread was constant.

They went for drives. Eddie lived out in the pastoral hills— horses, sheep, goats, verandas and koi ponds and stone fences skirting the edge of the rising and falling and rising land.

"I'd like to chase skirt, Van," Eddie said. "Like back in the day. But now I have a wife. I have a family. I know my priorities, man. Cost-benefit, and all that."

"Okay," Van said. "I see what you mean." Van wasn't sure why he told *him* this. Telling himself?

"I'm not perfect, so don't be in awe. Pedestals collect pigeon shit too, you know. You're not a bad guy because of this."

Eddie told Van he tried to set Van up with his wife's cousin—his cousin through marriage. Try something new, something different. Get yourself back out there. Don't rest on your laurels.

"Worth a shot."

A week later she called.

They met for ice cream, but she was too much for Van. Van felt inferior—she had a graduate degree, owned her own home. Her watch was worth more than Van's station wagon.

"I played in the bigs with Eddie. That's how we know each other," Van said.

Her name was Christina. She looked at him as if he just announced he secretly was an iguana.

"I know all about that…of course," she said. "I'm in the family."

"I forgot."

Van poked his spoon at the empty paper bowl.

He knew she thought he was a complete oddball.

There's nothing I can do about the way people think or feel, Van thought.

"It's better that I'm off on my own right now," Van said. "Don't want to burden anybody."

"You're not a weight, man."

But Van was gone the next day. His station wagon was not exactly ancient, but it already rattled and sounded queasy. He couldn't even afford to buy a decent car. Talk about a hole in the confidence department.

The Time Van Imagined His Funeral

It would be well-attended—all my ex-teammates and friends and family members. The church would have a white steeple right by the water. Birds would chatter in the brush as the mourners entered.

Inside the church my remains would rest in an urn next to the podium where mourners would chant poems by Auden and Yeats from dog-eared volumes. They would say glowing things about me—as a baseball player ("very good; not the greatest; career cut short by injury, but very, very good") as a father ("kind and generous and always loving") as a friend ("what a great listener") as a husband ("always an endearing partner for life; we will miss him terribly").

The music would be Bach.

The flowers would be irises—purple and pale purple and blue. Glistening with dewdrops.

The temperature would be 70 degrees and dry, not a cloud in the sky. A light wind would bounce the leaves.

As for the burial, my remains would be slowly, dramatically lowered into the casket, then slowly, dramatically lowered into the earth. Thousands of flowers would shower upon my casket and the people I loved and who loved me would tear and wail and several would rend at their clothes.

The mourners would slowly toss dirt onto my casket.

The birds would chirp. The sun would shine. The earth would cool.

51

Off and on Van worked on decks. Usually he was the guy to hold the two by four, to fetch more nails, to stain the deck when it was all done. Michael Foster told Van he always had a job with Foster and Sons. Always. That's the way it worked out.

Michael's sons Max and Berry were the sons. They did the bulk of the work. Van played the role of the grunt, that was clear. But Van could handle that. He was not too proud for sweat. Michael Foster wore gold necklaces and t-shirts advertising beer and big class rings on both hands. Max and Berry slicked their hair back with product and cussed every other word.

Nobody asked him about the bigs. A long time ago. Cheryl had either neglected to mention it to Michael or didn't think it relevant. Van thought it might help him get an edge and wish he would at least get a nod, a mention—something. He often felt overlooked, in the shadows.

They should cut him a break, he thought. He didn't want to put himself in a pickle though. Michael seemed testy and often easily offended. He avoided mentioning much about his past unless pressed.

Most days he felt grateful to have a job. Even if everything else went sour, he could still use his hands.

Michael Foster, however, wasn't Van's kind of guy. He was stiff-lipped and rigid. Stoic. Van saw where he fit in the hierarchy, but it existed as an unrelenting caste system without much give.

53

"I have experience," Van told him, but the preconceptions stuck.

His knee started to hurt. Van knew he needed to see someone again, maybe return to physical therapy. Something to cut through the never-ending pain. Difficult enough to meet the $750 rent, plus utilities. He barely squeaked by as it was, and Van knew his diet of pasta and canned spaghetti sauce would soon get old.

But his knee ached and pounded with pain. When the ice fell from the sky. When the sun blared. Sometimes, for no reason at all. He watched Michael eyeball him—as if because of his limp Van couldn't be trusted. As if he were less of a man.

"Are you *okay?*"

As if having a limp equals a moral failing. As if having a bum knee made him a bum. As if he were a cripple, some kind of wayward bum gimp.

"Four operations," Van said. Keep it factual, Van said, not emotional. "Doing the best I can."

He carried the box of nails and two by fours through the grass. Max and Berry blasted Boston and Led Zeppelin, and he walked around shirtless and drank beer. He kept to himself and did what he was told.

At lunch breaks Max would pry. Nobody taught him it was rude. Berry seemed more accepting, though also angrier when the ball didn't bounce his way (he was younger, shorter, less handsome).

"Do you still talk to your old family?" Max smirked. Van didn't understand why he smirked. Was there something wrong with his face? Did he find Van's situation outlandish in some way?

"They're still my family," Van said. "I have two kids."

"But if they're still your family, then you're living with them, right?"

"I'm taking a break."

"Taking a break from family? How does *that* work?"

This is what he didn't like. The questions. The judgments.

Van ate his peanut butter sandwich and didn't say a thing.

"How does that work, Van?"

Van's knee throbbed. He popped pain killers. At home a frozen bag of spinach sat in the freezer, and he wished he could somehow call on some Popeye power.

Need to go back to the basics, Van thought. He felt stretched-out, unmoored from what he knew.

He quit the job.

Michael complained and moaned. He said Van left him in a horrible situation. "If I could punch you out, I would."

"Go ahead. You think I've never been punched before? That shit has happened a thousand times. I feel nothing."

Van couldn't find another job for months. The college kids had dibs on all the menial slots. He called numbers up and down the classifieds for months. Nothing.

Then unemployment checks that didn't cover his expenses. He hated doing it but he had to ring Cheryl and ask for a few hundred. She obliged.

"When are you going to come by and see your children? They'd love to see you."

"I can't be there right now," Van said. "You know that. Especially…"

He meant Timothy. Van knew he would likely never attain perfection, but he couldn't face down his replacement. He'd have to purge the contents of his innards first—not easy to greet with open arms.

Van even went door to door in the mall and in the "old towne" district. Nobody had work for him. Time to think outside the box, he thought.

That's when he stopped paying rent. A challenge to the universe, of sorts.

He recognized people there but hid his eyes. He saw those old neighbors—the ones with the cute girl. What was her name? Cheryl would know. Too many people he knew. Too much shame lurking around every corner.

He ducked into a toy store. Fiddled with the Match Box cars, waiting for something to happen.

50

"VB," The Handler said. "It's the books."

"Great news," Van said. "Just what I wanted to hear."

Van milked the dredges of his savings and he had no idea how. Life was expensive. He hated the efficiency with every morsel of his soul. The fluorescent ceiling lights. The grey industrial carpeting. The bland beige walls. The noises below him rumbling all day long—he lived above a coffee shop. When he signed the lease Van thought the notion appealing—the smell of freshly brewed coffee would alert him to his new position in life, his new reality. Instead, the coffee had a sour flavor—it smelled of cat piss, not the mountains of Sumatra.

The phone felt heavy in Van's hand. The Handler delivered all of his bad news that way, if he could help it—Van noticed. Van wondered if he did this so he could avoid physical repercussions, if it came to that. Confrontation averse.

"I haven't been telling you," The Handler said. "I didn't want you to worry."

"You didn't want me to *worry*? This stash is all I have left."

"It was built on a poor foundation," The Handler said. "That's all I'm trying to say."

"What do you mean? This was *your* suggestion. You pushed me into this, remember?"

He said Bistro Bistro was a sinking ship and there wasn't much Van could do about it. If anything. The bank clamped its jaws around it already.

"There will be an auction," the Handler said. "We'll try to recoup some losses there."

56

Van went. It took every bone in his body moving in the opposite direction they ordinarily would, but he did attend.

Bistro Bistro was a stupid name, Van thought. He never should've trusted Harry. Harry was the chef with the golden touch. Fool's gold, seemingly. Vultures—these men in suits crawling, picking their way through Bistro Bistro. Everything was for sale—the chairs, the tables, the cutlery, the ovens, the wine. The Bistro Bistro echoed as the auctioneer rattled off the dollar figures in rapid fire.

Twofiftyhavewegottwofiftytwofiftytwoseventyfivedowehavetwos eventyfivetwoseventyfivethreehundredistherethreehundred.

Van remembered the opening. It was only five years ago. How could that be? Time seemed elastic, seemed to escape him somewhere. It moved through him, past him. Josh and Ashley were just kids then. Cheryl wore her red and black silk dress. Expectation. Van's backers said he's had the best in town.

He still couldn't be sure what a bistro *was*, not exactly. Still. The Handler explained it to him and it sounded good, but what *was* a bistro anyway? Wasn't it just another word for restaurant? Was the Bistro Bistro a restaurant restaurant? He didn't like the name, but The Handler assured him the point rested in the emphasis. Mario said he didn't like it either, but he was just the chef. What did he know about such decisions?

The tables went, the stemware. The art went for peanuts.

The mirrors.

Tax write-off prices—hardly even worth the effort. He should have donated everything to Goodwill.

Van would still owe the bank $200,000 and change. And it would crush him. And he knew it.

The auctioneer's mouth rattled. Van watched the hole open and close, a line of saliva connecting the top and bottom walls of the cave. The suits adjusted their ties and smiles. The scavengers reveled at his pain. The Handler though—nowhere to be seen. Van thought this was odd since it was his doing. It was so bad The Handler wouldn't even call.

49

Van sat at Bistro Bistro, drinking an iced-tea.

"Hey, Chief," Mario said, brushing by.

The restaurant was empty, minus a few regular retirees who liked the omelets. It was twelve-thirty on a Thursday.

It had been two years since Cheryl left him, or he left Cheryl, or they left each other. In a way he felt a greater sense of calm. He was his own man again, for the first time in a decade plus. He missed the house; he missed his kids. But Cheryl—he rarely thought about her. That was a dead-end street for years. He just never realized it until it ended. Then he saw the opportunity.

Except now he needed to sell himself in a different way, and he felt zero confidence in it. But given how little Bistro Bistro offered him in income, he needed something else.

Real estate.

Spread in front of him on the table: listings—none of which enticed a single bite. The market was down, sure. But also he needed to be more proactive. He needed to get out there, spread the word. He used to stuff envelopes, send out fliers, make cold calls even. Van could still do these things, he just needed to summon the energy. He hoped staring at the listings might inspire him. He sucked from the iced tea and felt the cool air-conditioned air exhale against his cheek. How much am I wasting on energy bills? Van wondered.

He'd have to check in with The Handler on that. Why didn't he put his own name on the restaurant façade? Should they bank on his fame? He'd have to check in with The Handler on that, too. Excess treading of water.

He took out a notepad and began brainstorming:

--I feel desperate doing this shit.

--If the player's union looked out for us, I wouldn't have to.

--~~Buy property, rent it out~~. No. Too long-term.

--Lottery ticket?

--At least I only have myself to worry about.

--Fliers? Yes, but who to send them to? Worn out welcome?
~~You're such an idiot~~.

Was he flailing? He felt he was flailing.

48

"I really don't know where else to go," Van said.

Jarvis was a friend and he owned a bakery/convenience store. He confided in Van that he sold the lottery tickets and beer and condoms just to make the bread and cakes and pies feasible. So much didn't sell. So much waste.

"You know I have a cot in the back," Jarvis said.

"Do you mind?"

"Are you kidding me? I rarely use it." Jarvis said it was only if he had a run, or several cakes on morning order.

A tough time to be Van. His family disintegrated. *He* was in the process of disintegrating. He felt dusty and impermanent, like a withered piece of paper in some obscure bookstore—something hidden from the light and ignored, to be found by historians or archeologists from some distant year.

Van scrolled through his marriage in his head—back and forth, up and down—as if he had those ten years on a loop. He knew he was not exactly an ideal partner, but he also knew he did not deserve this treatment.

The cat squeaked beneath his weight. He felt adrift on a small raft of metal and fabric.

Jarvis baked and came and went. Van barely noticed.

"Would you like some food?"

Jarvis's forehead appeared gouged with deep wrinkles. His eyes revealed worry.

"I only crave pumpkin pie. Do you have any?"

Jarvis made one and an hour and a half later he brought Van a large wedge, still hot from the oven. The pie oozed with melted vanilla ice cream.

"For you, my friend."

Van ate the dripping wedge with his fingers and licked the crumbs from them. He thought of it as the most delicious thing he's ever eaten.

"Thank you," he said. "It's very good."

Van didn't want to talk. He only wanted to sleep, to hide away. One day led into the next.

He had no interest in dealing with the papers, lawyers.

Jarvis came in one morning.

"We should get you walking around," he said. "It's good for you to get some vitamin D."

"But where can I go?"

"Let's walk down to the lake. It's not too far."

"Isn't it several miles away? I mean…"

"It's not that far."

But it felt far. Van had a difficult time. He shuffled as Jarvis lead the way.

"You're not always kind to yourself," he said. "Don't beat on yourself up all the time."

Van watched his shoelaces bob as he walked. He had nothing to say and even if he did, he wasn't about to say it.

He nodded in affirmation.

"You've got an opportunity here to see things as they are. Clarity of thought is under-rated."

He nodded again. The sun felt warm against his skin. He felt like a prisoner set loose out into the world. Something newfound. Only he knew he would return to the cot in back in no time.

When Jarvis left, Van would smoke. He opened the back door to the bakery and waved the fumes away from the door. It was a little pleasure, something Cheryl would never approve of.

He smoked an entire pack one night, one right after the other. He put each nub out against the asphalt, collected the butts and later threw them in the Dumpster behind the grocery store next door. Nobody knew where he was and he liked that feeling. He liked that feeling a whole lot.

He must've deserved it on some level. On some level—otherwise it wouldn't have happened to him in the first place.

We get our just desserts, eventually. They stalk us, they hunt us down, they find us.

47

He felt paralyzed, unable to move. So he didn't move. Van slept in the guest room next door.

"Timothy's wife knows," Cheryl said. "So now *you* know and everything has to change. And I mean now."

"Oh," he said. "Nobody asked him for *permission*. What do you want exactly?"

"Nothing. I don't want anything. It was just…."

Van could barely look at Cheryl during the teary exchange. He felt zero desire to deal with the after-effects of something he didn't create. Destruction. Devastation.

He knows he should be angry or curious about Timothy. Some men might find a weapon. Van felt simply too stunned to think or move. He just wanted to rest, to let things sink in.

In the room next to him (his old bedroom) he could hear arguments, crying, the manic squeaking of bedsprings.

"Shouldn't we at least….for the sake of decency?"

But nobody paid him any mind. They were in *heat*.

Joshua and Ashley spent the week at summer camp. The frogs croaked at night, moths pinged against the outdoor lamps. He could smell citronella in the air as if it emanated from the thick clouds themselves.

After several days of this, Cheryl came to him.

"There's nothing for you to do," she said. "We need arrangements. That's pretty much it."

So they split. Cheryl wrote him a fat check for his half of the house, plus a little more. She said she'd like the children to stay with her, for the sake of continuity. It had the feel of a dream, an unreality which slow-dripped into him despite himself.

"What did I do?" Van asked. It *leaked* out of him, more than anything. From his gut. "I mean, what did I do to *you*?"

"You were fine. This is. This is just one of those unfortunate things. It's bad luck for you, I know that. I know you were faithful. I know that too. There's just not enough *fight* in you. It's like you're treading water. You're going against yourself all the time."

Van wished it otherwise. How can luck actually change? What might precipitate that? It was a problem. It was *the* problem of his life. He was cursed—or felt he was cursed, which made it so. Feeling cursed and *being* cursed are seemingly one and the same. When does it become self-fulfilling?

"I should leave you two," Van said.

"That would be best," Cheryl said. Her face flushed and she couldn't look at Van. "Just so you know, I didn't plan for this to happen."

She kept it factual and on-the-surface. Cheryl felt little need to discuss abstractions, to analyze human connection, or lack thereof. She said it didn't really amount to much.

Perhaps she was, on some level, superficial. Something Van had no desire to admit.

"The children come home from camp soon," Cheryl said. He knew this. "They come back in a few days. We'll talk with them together, the way it should be."

No way Van could ever do that, he knew. He couldn't face down their disappointment in him. He couldn't bear witness to their developing rage, to their future selves. *That* Cheryl would have to deal with. Alone, or with Timothy.

In the guest room Van watched a camelback cricket fling itself against a wall. Cricket trap under the bed, but the insect hadn't stumbled his way to it. Van watched the cricket's animal idiocy. His legs compressed and released and the cricket sprung into the air, bumping into the yellow painted ball.

Van packed a suitcase of clothes. Everything else he left behind. Remnants from another life.

The Time Van and Cheryl Fought all Night Long

It was an epic fight that started, of course, with an idiotic, pointless trigger. Ashley slept over at a friend's house and Josh stayed at his grandparents' for the night, so we had the place to ourselves.

We decided to live it up and cook a gourmet meal, settle down with a movie. She decided on veal parmesan, plus asparagus, plus this potato casserole thing, which sounded too heavy to me, but I went along with it. Cheryl was the acting captain of that ship and I just went along with the plan and tried to help where I could.

I was in the middle of chopping onions for the potato casserole when she said: "No, *dice* them. They need to be smaller, please."

And if she had just said that it would have been fine. But in the next breath she mumbles: "Don't you *know* anything?"

As soon as she said it, I could tell she regretted it. It was unnecessary, out of the ordinary. I should have left it there, knowing that—I should've taken the high road, knowing that she didn't mean it to sound as harsh as it did. But something in me couldn't keep it in.

She lit into this whole speech about how when she met me she thought I was such as stud, so filled with confidence and vigor, and I seemed well-connected and successful and stable. Instead, I remained jobless, living off my savings and what pension I got. What had *happened* to me? Where had the younger Van gone? What happened to my mojo?

This ballooned out of control. The food tasted terrible—burnt or overcooked as a result of our argument. At one point I chased her from room to room, questioning her attacks. At another point she shoved me against the sofa.

"Just get a damn job," she said. "Be *productive* for once. Work."

"I had a job. I *was* a ballplayer," I said. "As you know."

"*Was*," she said. "Past. Tense. *Was*. Was, was, was. You are a *was*."

Neither of us could sleep. One of the worst nights of my life.

It took me three sleeping pills to finally knock myself out. I woke up a loser.

46

The week before the big party nothing worked. The purpose of the party? To celebrate Cheryl's fortieth—a "monumental" birthday, in her words. For years she had talked about having a big blow-out. "If I'm going down, we're going to celebrate. Her family, all her friends, her colleagues, neighbors, everybody would be there. She wanted to face it down in style, she said.

It started with the clogged basement toilet—Drano failed to work, neither did plunging. Nothing seemed to clear it. Then it was the dishwasher, which leaked and left plates and cups and silverware *dirtier* somehow, after a so-called washing than they were to begin with. The cable went out next, and the computers ceased functioning. The microwave would churn but wouldn't heat. The two overhead fans made weird insect-like clicking noises. The electrical sockets in the living room sparked and the air conditioning only emitted luke-warm, noxious air. On top of it all Van's new station wagon failed to start.

Van and Cheryl owned a beautiful home in a beautiful neighborhood and nothing was the way it should be.

64

All that week Van pressed the phone to his ear—repairmen, meeting with plumbers and electricians and cable guys and car mechanics. A shit storm of epic proportions.

But slowly the men made repairs and restored sanity and Van could progress to the matter-at-hand—preparing for his wife's 40th shindig. Luckily, he didn't have to worry about the food—the guys from Bistro Bistro had that taken care of, with a menu requested by Cheryl and an open bar to keep the adults happy.

The day of the party Van kept himself busy with yard work, helping the Bistro guys set up chairs and tables in the yard, setting up the volleyball net, and horseshoes and badminton. Van was thorough, scouring the places the cleaning ladies missed, remulching the yard, trimming. He took Q-tips and expunged the residue from the refrigerator crevices. He dusted the overhead fan blades. He washed windows.

The Bistro Bistro crew seemed in top shape, despite the cutbacks. Mario made delicious quiche and ribs and stuffed zucchini and Greek salad. The Handler knew a guy who knew a guy who knew a top D.J. The speakers and subwoofers were almost too powerful, but the D.J. took requests with ease and he played the set list, which Cheryl loved. During every other song she lifted her head and said, "Oh, my. I love this song. *I have* to dance!"

Ted and Eileen and Fred and Cal and Tracy were all there from the neighborhood and Grover dropped by later with his daughters and his mom, who visited from Colorado. Cheryl's colleagues had a blast—truly letting their hair down. Van had never met most of them prior—only Gail plus a few quick phone conversations with Ellen. Van liked Gail's boss, Mr. Jerkins, right away (hearty sense of humor) and Ed and Bobby seemed like a friendly lot—unpretentious if a bit on the slovenly side. But Van spent more time talking to Timothy, a new "project manager" (self-described). According to Cheryl he could be a real go-getter, up and coming. Tall and tan and his teeth emanated a lustrous white glow, which reminded Van of starlight. They talked baseball—though didn't mention his playing days (if he had....) Timothy discussed the benefits of the designated hitter. "I don't want to see the *pitcher* hit. It never really works).

At the conclusion of their conversation, Timothy slapped Van on the back and said, "You've got a hell of a home, hell of a wife. You're one lucky man." And he glided off for another glass of red.

As for Cheryl's friends and family—it was the usual crew: her parents and sister, plus the kids. Her cousin Ken brought a friend and Cheryl's old college pals were there, along with her workout partner, her vacation buddy, the ladies from the book club (or most of them) and Harriet, who went back to Cheryl's third grade class.

By two in the morning everyone packed it in and Cheryl kissed Van on the cheek and said it was a "Special night, unforgettable." She cooed: he always looking out for her—that's why she loved him.

"There are a lot of people who love you," Van said. "As evidenced by the great turnout."

"That was all you," she said. "You rallied the troops."

With everything he'd been through recently, it felt like *his* celebration as much as hers.

They made love on the floor. The shadows created an interesting lattice work on the bedspread, as if it were sheathed in a grid pattern, a chess board.

"You make me happy," she said.

An owl hooted as they slept. It sounded like a cry of distress, a warning. It registered to Van as a dream. He slept.

The Time Van Wept in the Tub, Part 3

I wasn't sure why. I took a bath and it just came tumbling out of me, stunned. I was a shabby father, a subpar provider, lover, friend and son and everything I did came out half-baked and ill-conceived. Unfinished. I realized if I plunked The Handler down into my roll even he'd probably do a better job.

I draped two ratty washcloths over my head and bawled and blubbered.

Cheryl and the kids ventured out looking for school supplies and clothes.

I was completely *disconnected*. I was not the man I wanted to be.

My knee left me a quasi-cripple. I needed a job but I was floundering.

I splashed water on my face and toweled off and I got dressed somehow and eventually Cheryl and the kids pulled in. I slapped my face.

"Hey gang," I said. Smiling. I tried to.

45

When Van's father sat in the ICU Van took Ashley and Josh to the zoo. He had been to visit his father every day for the past week and the doctors said he had little chance to recover. "It has metastasized. At this point it's merely a waiting game." How many times over their careers have the doctors reiterated those exact lines? "A waiting game." Did they mimic the doctors on TV or did the doctors on TV mimic them? It must be rote by now, a conveyor belt of death sentences.

The zoo seemed larger than Van remembered—he hadn't been for years and years. With Joshua's interest in science and Ashley's love of animals Van thought it a natural fit for a day of relaxation.

"What do you want to see first? The giraffes? The big cats? The boa constrictors?" Van held the map in front of him

Joshua shrugged and Ashley looked off at the foliage outside the zoo.

"Is Granddad dying?" Ashley asked. She didn't look at Van.

"I don't really know. It's always possible. But they're hopeful." The lie was to himself as much as anything.

"Why don't we just start at the beginning of the map and we'll wend our way back?"

"That's original," Josh said. "Nobody else will be doing that."

The teenage years. Tough on us all, Van thought.

"Okay," Van said. "Then it's reptiles."

Inside the reptile house the lighting seemed dim and obscure. A refreshing change of pace from the gleaming sheen of the hospital. Was the ever present white an attempt to sidetrack us?

Josh and Ashley hustled ahead. Van lingered from tank to tank inspecting each specimen—the corn snake, the king snake, the python, the snapping turtle tank, the desert lizards, the Gila monster. Van fixated on the measured pacing of the Gila monster. He must've stood in front of the tank for fifteen minutes. Watching him (her?) trek steadily to one side of the tank and then back, tongue flogging the air every so often.

Shit, Van thought, the kids.

Van raced through the remainder of tanks and came out the other side, but neither Ashley nor Josh could be seen. Where were they? He walked down the lion paw-print path, hoping to catch up to them. Nothing doing. After some coffee-klatch voice bleated their names on the intercom system, the kids finally emerged—ice cream cones and sodas in hand, contrite.

"We lost track of time," Joshua said.

Van ripped into them hard. He told them that their mother would hear about this little ploy. He knew that teenagers were rebellious by nature and not as liable to injury or kidnap as someone say ten and under. Still, Van felt the weight of responsibility.

"You stay with me from now on. I know you're older now. But still. I need to keep everyone together."

"Okay, Dad," Joshua said.

"Is there something wrong?" Van asked.

"I don't know," Joshua said.

"You seem kinda tense," Ashley said.

Van said that he *was* tense, but that he's trying not to be, and that he's trying to forget the worst of everything. He knew his father was dying and that he tried to distract himself from that. Plus, spending some time with his children—he thought the zoo a good idea. Was it? Perhaps it could be a kind of fatherly formula. Perhaps *he* was a fatherly formula.

"Let's just go and see the next thing," Ashley said.

The kids acted as an instrument of measurement, a reflection of his best and worst moments.

They saw the flamingos.

They saw the tropical birds.

They saw the antelope and water buffalo and zebras and giraffes stooping and craning.

"It's tragic," Ashley said. "They have nothing and they're in prison."

"It's one way to look at it," Van said.

Josh kept his hands in his pockets, chewing on his bubble gum. Where he acquired the gum Van had no idea.

"What other way is there? They can't roam. They're just stuck here. They're probably all depressed. Dad, is this where *you* wanted to go to cheer up? You've *got* to be kidding."

Van felt as if someone handed him a script he'd read before. It all sounded familiar.

They had stopped moving. They stood on a giant bear paw painted in huge black and red prints on the sidewalk.

"What do you think, Josh?"

"I don't know," he said. "We're all going down eventually, right? At least they have someone to give them food and stuff."

"That's an excellent point, Josh. Very good."

Ashley rolled her eyes and shook out her hair.

"Maybe the bears and tigers will change your mind," Van said. "Those are animals that could kill the hell out of you."

Van loved his children, but sometimes he felt his love orbiting around him like a distant moon. How devoted to them *was* he? Would he really and truly do *anything* for his children? He didn't know. He knew he loved them, but how much? How could he *quantify* the love?

69

Back at the hospital he held his father's hand. His father seemed to register Van's presence with a quick flicker of his eyelids. Perhaps, however, he just dreamed or remembered some young lady from before he met mom, or perhaps he fantasized of a juicy steak or walking along the beach at night. Who knows?

Two weeks later his father dissipated. The doctors said he did well to make it that far. Van would bury him next to Mom in the old cemetery—he knew that. He'd never want to be laid to rest there himself—too close to the highway; too congested with death. Van would want to return to the forest somewhere, die amongst the trees, have squawking birds carry him away one bit at a time, ingest him one bit at a time, fly over the mountains with pieces of him propelling them.

The Time Josh's Friends Made Van Tell Them about Playing Professional Baseball

Josh and his two friends Brent and Eddie messed around in the basement. I sat upstairs stuffing envelopes with real estate fliers.

"No way," one of the kids said.

"Go ask him," Josh said.

They scrambled up the stairs.

"Josh says you played pro baseball. He is lying, right?"

I didn't say anything.

"Dad," Josh said.

"He's not lying," I said.

It was like the press room, only with teenage boys.

They wanted to know everything—what it felt like to play in Fenway Park, which famous players I knew, did I go to the All-Star game, did I meet Babe Ruth. Yankee Stadium. Mickey Mantle. Ty Cobb. Endless. One of these days I should write a book, I thought. Just to save myself time.

"You like baseball, right?"

"Yeah, yeah, yeah." They seemed eager, grasping for answers.

"The best thing I can do or say is it was a great experience and I'm lucky—or was lucky. But there's no way I can capture it all. It's impossible. You had to be there."

The questions continued, but I lied and said I needed to vacuum out my car. I walked outside to the garage and they followed me. But I wouldn't say anything else on the matter. When the vacuum clicked on, I could only hear the voices in my head.

44

"I know exactly who you are," the man said. Van shuffled his feet in the little bakery. A new one. "I was a huge fan back in the day. Are you *kidding* me?"

"It's nothing," Van said. "You know what happened to my career."

"Yeah, but you were a shining star. You were like a mayfly— short lived, but man you could play some ball back in the day."

Van winced.

"I'm sorry, I don't mean to compare you to an insect."

"No, I know what you mean. It's okay." Van always acted flattered when someone remembered him, even if Major League Baseball itself seemed ambivalent. His average salary was that of a mid-range lawyer. He wasn't rich. He did okay, but if his restaurant slipped a bit, if he didn't sell any houses.

"My name is Jarvis Keegan," the man said. "I wish I had something for you to autograph!"

"Nice to meet you."

Jarvis told Van he just moved to Maryland from New York—too cut-throat there. He hoped he could start afresh here—mellow and relaxed. New place, new life.

"I like the trees," Jarvis said. He felt optimistic; Van liked that. He gravitated to those who looked at the upside. Van didn't, not always. It seemed fake. He needed to learn that.

Van felt good about his life, at that moment. His restaurant was doing well—as well as could be expected for a new bistro with a bad name.

His real estate venture seemed to be on the upswing, even though he was new to it. He had a new car—a multi-purpose station wagon, highly functional. He underwent a positive transition.

What is normalcy? Van wondered. Does the status quo even exist? His life already had so many unexpected twists. His old normalcy seemed so far away. What would his new normalcy look like? Is this it? Restaurateur and real estate pusher? Some part of Van distrusted appearances. Stability seemed elusive. Were the best years in his life behind him? Or ahead of him?

Van drove to the intersection of Vine and Route 55. It was a beautiful June day, the light sieving through the maples and tulip poplars. A man hobbled down the median with a bucket. He wore a sign which read: "Please help—hungry and wounded." It's not the best place for a pan handler, Van thought. He tried to take a left and at any point a driver distracted by the bum might cause the others to miss the light. Just for that, you're getting nothing. He rolled up his window and glared at the guy. Idiot.

Van turned up the music in his new car. It didn't possess a great sound system, but he supposed it was good enough. The car still had that rubbery fresh car smell—who didn't love that?

Van drove by one of his listed houses and another one which had an open house on Saturday. That should be an easy sell, he thought. He stopped and bought a bottle of apple juice at the convenience store and he drank it in the parking lot alone. The coldness and the sugar helped him.

Van thought about his father. He knew he should call him back. He forgot. His father didn't sound so great on the message. Congested or something. Van drove out into the countryside, away from the houses. He loved that driving twenty minutes allowed him a respite from people and talking and the stresses of suburban life. There was something serene about farms and charming little produce stands and snowball shops.

He drove just to drive.

That Jarvis guy, Van thought. He seems like a decent sort. I think I could be friends with a guy like him, Van thought. I could use a few— even Cheryl has said so. It would be good to have a guy nearby to drink a beer with, to talk about worldly troubles.

Van kept driving west. Route 55 narrowed to a one lane road and the farms became more sporadic. He saw a house farm there, then a sod farm, a cluster of houses, then open woods. Someday Van would like to own a place in the woods somewhere—to get away from it all. Just like when he was a little tyke.

He wondered if Cheryl would go for it—she might get bored.

When he came across a real estate sign advertising a plot of ten wooded acres, he stopped and trudged back through the grass to the edge of the copse. It smelled fresh out there, idyllic really. He knew he should be wary of idealizing, but still.

Van wrote down the number. A possibility.

He'd call the agent that night—just an inquiry. Nothing wrong with that.

But by the time he returned home he shuffled onto something else, and someone needed to cut the lawn.

The Time Van Sabotaged his Chances to Make a Bunch of Money

The Handler told me about the IPO. He claimed the company was the next big thing, his guy on the inside said so and The Handler trusted him. He put his own money into the company. Twenty grand, thirty grand, a hundred grand. Everybody was. So I should as well.

"You should put at least ten grand in," he said. "You'll at least double your money by July, I guarantee. Snagging candy from a toddler."

73

"Let me think about it," I said.

Hesitation: my usual way of saying no. And this seemed no different. I didn't actually decide anything; I said maybe and then forgot to get back to him. Very passive-aggressive.

My mistake. Big mistake.

The Handler bought shares of the company's IPO for $40. Two years later it was $360. I would've made $100,000 easy.

Instead, I hemmed and hawed, chickened out of my own possible success.

I took risks in life. They just always seem to be the wrong risks.

43

Van often woke up with an aching feeling of dread—the same feeling he had when he came to bat against a pitcher he just knew had his number for one reason or another. He was out before he even swung at the pitch.

The year Van's mother died, he often awoke in an idyllic haze. He had beautiful dreams of gardens and piercing blue waters and peonies falling from the sky and landing at his feet. In his dreams he fantasized he circles of beautiful ladies surrounded him—the kind who flocked most often to his teammates when he was a ball player. But innocent. Often his dreams were so pleasant he had no desire to wake up.

"Son, why don't you come over? Your mother needs your help." Van's father on the phone. Voice hoarse.

He never uttered "son." Something must be wrong, Van thought.

"Sure, what with?"

"Some cleaning out. She has a project. You know how that goes."

When Van arrived, his mother embraced him—also unusual. His family did not consist of huggers.

"Would you mind emptying your old room? It's been a while and we could really use the extra storage space, you know. We're not getting any younger."

"Oh, sure."

But first she fed him, as she always did. Grilled cheese and tomato and potato chips. Celery and peanut butter. His mother knew her fallbacks, her go-tos. He drank lemon water, just like when he was a boy. Little seeds floating amongst the ice cubes.

"Yeah, we're trying to declutter is all."

She washed the dishes as he ate. Her back to him. He watched it, the slight resigned hunch in it. Van did not believe anything was terribly wrong.

"It's a long life," she said.

They kept his room as it appeared when he was twenty-seven, when his playing days ended. Fixed in time, as if he had died, as if on display in a museum. His equipment, remnants. Everything.

On his dresser rested the trophies—the one golden glove award, the American league champion plaque, the smaller ones from the minors. His old gloves fanned out on the bookcase—like magazines in a doctor's office waiting room—from little league to the bigs. Several of his uniforms hung framed on the wall. Five bats leaned against the closet. The balls sat in a glass case—his first hit, several from the playoffs, a few he got autographed when he was a young player. His parents maintained his little museum all these years, devoted fans in their own way. Her way. Everything dusted, crisp.

Van stood at the threshold, taking it all in. On some level he knew it was time—Mom was right. The end was pain; he had forgotten how much he accomplished. Van needed to remember, count his blessings. He needed a mantra. His mother implicitly told him that he needed to hold on to that, to keep it present and living within him. He often moved on to new things—investments, his livelihood, Ashley, Josh, his home and marriage and life.

The Handler helped him get a deal on the Mercedes—otherwise he never could have afforded it. The vehicle sputtered on its last legs and

Van was already of a mind to purchase something more practical: a mini-van. Perhaps a station wagon.

He loaded it up with his baseball career—the leftovers of it.

Van would leave his little league glove with his father. Van knew he would want that for his grandchildren to see. Later he would return and pick up any leftover items still remaining.

But by the time he remembered, his mother had already passed on. She went in her sleep—"painless," his father said. Whatever that meant—was anything ever painless? His father's hands trembled when he said it. One hand braced the other. Van watched it all.

42

Cheryl seemed restless. She usually did: so many things to do and so little time. Van watched her as if from afar. A balmy air wafted through the windows. Cheryl checked duties from her list.

"We have money. We can hire someone for that," Van said. But inside he knew that he was likely the cause of the restlessness—his stubbornness, intractability.

"For what?"

"You know, the little chores and things."

"We *don't* have the money."

Van shrugged. He knew she was right. They didn't. At one point they probably did, but Van had drained much of his savings. The Handler said he was still in good shape with investments—stocks and bonds. Plus, he had the house and the condo on the shore. He could sell that if he ever needed to.

"I'm heading out," she said. Her flip-flops made an insistent beat as she grabbed her keys, her purse. Aren't flip flops supposed to send *calming* vibes?

"You're picking up Ashley from softball, right?"

"Thought you were up this week."

"No, it's you."

"Jesus."

"I'm taking Josh to David's, remember?"

"Can't you pick up Ashley afterwards?"

Always who was driving, kid chauffer duty.

Cheryl stood at the door, her foot tapping in annoyance. Sometimes Van thought her hobby was getting things done. He appreciated the meticulousness, and she was nothing if not attentive, but he wished for just a bit more lassitude. Maybe a vacation now and then. Perhaps this is why she considered baseball to be "dull." She couldn't sit still long enough.

He reminded Cheryl that David's house lay forty-five minutes from the softball fields.

"So leave a bit early then!"

She slammed the door behind her.

Van didn't mind these minor conflicts—at least *he* considered them minor. He knew Cheryl would apologize later and explain the numerous points on her list. "I just felt overwhelmed," she admitted.

The rotation of chores seemed sometimes so intricate Van wished he had a scorecard and a quality play-by-play guy.

They hadn't fucked in months.

"Make love," she'd correct him. He hated her corrections most of all. Her so-called purity.

"I don't make love. I make whoopee," Van joked. An ongoing dispute.

"You don't make love?"

"I love you always. I don't have to *make* it. That sounds as though I don't love you the times when I'm *not* making it."

"Don't be like that," she'd say. "I hate when you split hairs."

Van knew he needed a job, a hobby. Something to distract himself, something to fill a few hours of time a week. His knee throbbed constantly (he just hoped he didn't require yet another surgery). It didn't take much for boredom to occupy his mind. And if Van was bored, what about Cheryl?

When he picked up Ashley they talked about her at bats. She went one for four, a hard single to left.

"That's a good day," Van said.

"It's .250. That sucks. Below average."

"It's solid though. Any day you get a hit is a good day. Even days when you don't if you help out the team. Move a runner over, sac fly. Just being, sometimes. The grind."

When they got back Ashley took a nap, explaining that the sun got to her.

Van reclined on the sectional downstairs and propped up his knee on three pillow. Sometimes he wished they would just cut it off right above the knee cap. He could get used to half a wooden leg, or even the nothingness there. He could get used to anything.

41

Van wanted to take Ashley and Josh camping. A "rite of passage," he told Cheryl. "Just me and the kids."

"I can't come?"

"Do you want to?"

"No, but still."

"I know how you feel…"

"It would be nice….never mind."

Cheryl hated camping, said it felt like forced fun. Ashley and Josh had never been and Van believed they should. I spent a lot of time in the woods as a child," Van explained. "It's something that can help them through life. It's good for their souls.

"All true," Cheryl said. "Enjoy. I hope it stays dry."

Van picked an overnight in the foothills of West Virginia as his destination. Something felt familiar about that location. He let Ashley and Josh help. Josh was a bit young to understand the nuance of elevation, but he knew what he wanted to eat: s'mores, hot dogs on a stick, roasted apples (Van couldn't be sure where he got that last idea). Van had never seen Josh as happy as he was when they strolled through the grocery store planning their camping meals.

"Whatever you kids want," Van said. "It's fine with me."

When they pulled into the campsite Van thought it would be a terrific trip. It was in the middle of the week so the campsite seemed deserted. The bathrooms seemed relatively clean and equipped with showers. Mountains rose from the site and wild rhododendrons and mountain laurel and spruce peppered the hills. The old trees would be there long after he was no longer.

They set up camp. Josh held the tent in place while Ashley pounded stakes into the ground. Van aired out the musty interior and unrolled their sleeping bags.

Later they hiked down a switchback and up through a ravine and toward the mountain opposite. The rain began. At first a misty drizzle fell, but the farther the three hiked on the trail, the more the rain intensified.

"This sucks," Ashley said, her boot squelching mud.

"I'm soaked," Josh said.

Josh said they should head back, but he stayed optimistic that the tent would stay dry. They pitched it under a tree after all. Even though they were soaked, Van remained upbeat. He knew if he acted negative, they would too. They'd feed off him.

"Think about those delicious hot dogs we have waiting for us," Van said. "Something to look forward to."

But when they returned to the campsite they found the tent and everything inside of it soaked—the pillows, the sleeping bags, everything. And it still poured.

"If it stops raining maybe we can air everything out," Ashley said.

Josh looked forlorn.

"Everything is really wet," he said.

"Not the food—that's still in the trunk," Van said.

79

Ashley and Josh sat in the car, wet, as Van cooked hot dogs on the propane grill (thank God Van didn't rely on charcoal this time). He even roasted halved apples.

"My butt is really wet," Josh said. "I feel like a soggy noodle."

Van handed them both a paper plate with apples and a pile of potato chips and a hot dog in a bun.

They ate in the car as the rain pinged the windshield.

"We can sleep here," Van said. "It's not camping but it's *like* camping. We'd still be out in the woods."

"Let's go home, Dad," Ashley said.

The dark descended and the rain increased in intensity, if anything.

"Are you sure? Still not that bad."

"I want to be dry," Josh said. As quickly as they could they dismantled the wet tent and balled it into the trunk with the sleeping bags and sodden pillows.

Van drove them home. Ashely and Josh slept in their wet clothes as Van blasted the heater. He played the disco station softly, which reminded him of better times. It was a long, wet drive back and Van felt he had failed them in some way. He couldn't help it. He knew the weather spun out of control, but he felt he could have done better anyway. Somehow.

The windshield wipers flopped at full bore. Nothing ever matched expectations, Van thought. Nothing ever worked out the way it should. Nothing.

The Time Van had a Premonition

I hobbled through the grocery store in the produce section, squeezing the kiwis, feeling the fuzzy skin bristle against my fingertips. Cheryl wanted to make a fruit salad for brunch and she set me forth to purchase the goods. Her parents were coming over with her sister and her sister's kids and their dogs and I couldn't stand the dogs, which yipped and shat everywhere and my outlook on the dogs carried over to the kids and traveled north to the adults. I dreaded the whole thing and what made matters worse was the fact that I didn't know what a ripe kiwi felt like.

I saw a different life, one in which I subsisted alone and desperate. But it was on my terms. I stood in the middle of a field, insects buzzing around me, nobody around. I could breathe. I could envision this. Maybe I even wanted it.

I bagged six kiwis and moved on to the mangos. I stepped back into reality.

40

It was lunchtime so they went to Kent's. The Handler's favorite sandwich place. The Handler ordered a Reuben and Van got the turkey club. They sat in the far corner near the bathrooms, away from everybody.

"You're bleeding cash," The Handler said. "To be blunt. I'm sorry to have to put it to you that way. You still have plenty of savings. But...."

He took a big bite of his sandwich, dressing on his chin.

"I figured as much," Van said. "I know."

"You're spending way more money than you're making. That's the big problem for many ex-athletes in retirement. This is so common, so please don't worry. You aren't the only one. I mean, it's tough. You get used to a certain routine...This is a common occurrence."

The Handler told Van he needed income flow. He needed a job. He needed to do more with his investments. Perhaps start a business. He needed to think long term, to think smart.

It's paralyzing, Van thought. All of this. I don't know what to *do*.

"We need to find you an income flow."

Van's knee throbbed. He could still be playing. If he had the big name he'd be an announcer, something. If only his knee gave him five more years.

"Have confidence," The Handler said. "Be positive." He licked his fingers.

They strategized. Van could go all in on investments—the stock market, most notably. He could open a sports bar. Take some risks, reap the reward. You have the money, The Handler argued. Don't just sit on it—then you are losing money, losing opportunity.

"I don't drink though," Van reminded him. He could start a consulting firm. "What would I consult? I'm not an expert in anything." He could get a job—but what would he do? Work in a cubicle somewhere? In a factory? That seemed impossible.

He had no marketable skills.

"I have a job. Why couldn't you? It's normal. We need the income."

The Handler snapped off half of the dill pickle in his mouth.

Van lacked an answer.

"If we don't find something, you'll run out of money eventually. You will."

Van looked at the smudged bathroom door. All these hands which had pushed it open. He took his first bite of the club. He liked their sandwiches. He could do food, he thought. He'd figure something out.

"We have time," Van said.

"Okay, I mean—you're the boss. You are.

39

Van knew. He wasn't *completely* friendless exactly, but he certainly lacked friends. No doubt about that. He could count his true friends on one hand, in fact: Silver, Davy from school, and recently he had become friendly with Bill and Karen, Josh's friends' parents—they came over for dinner a few times and they went bowling once. But friendly didn't necessarily equal friends, someone you can confide in and trust. He knew little about them when it came down to it. They never helped him out in a pinch or saw him angry or flustered or saw him sob in the corner or discussed his hopes and anxieties and embarrassing foibles.

Van most fully felt middle-aged when he slumped in the bleachers to watch Ashley's softball games. He sat there on the hot aluminum, making small talk with the parents of his daughter's teammates, a dismal exercise. He wanted to tell them his full story, but he felt it would be gloating or perhaps self-pitying, and he really had no interest in being *that* guy.

But having kids seemed a good entryway into possible friendships. Cheryl reminded him that he should cultivate these.

"Someday you'll need someone. You'll want help."

"That's not all a friendship is about," he responded. "It's not as if all a friend is is someone to do a solid for you." They drove to look at potential new kitchen tiles at Ceramics Unleashed.

"What *is* it about then?"

"It's sharing something....it's about childhood and growing up together."

"Is that why you don't have more friends? Adults can still be friends. You didn't meet Silver when you were a kid."

"I was young though. And we were on a team. We were co-workers."

Cheryl suggested he get a hobby—some way to meet people. He'd make friends that way.

"What about adult softball?"

"You know that's not going to happen."

"Okay. You have *other* interests. Hell, bowling league or something."

Van looked down at the bleachers, at the grass underneath. It looked like a miniature version of the lakeside bleachers. He missed those times. Those times when everything spread in front of him wide open with possibility. At thirty-nine nothing seemed to *happen*. He was in the middle of it. His kids were growing up; he read the newspaper; events

83

took place elsewhere. Like a stagnant pool, his life just sat there, without a ripple. No breeze. No movement.

Van didn't have friends because he didn't want any. Who would want to share *this* with him? Nothing *to* share. It was birthday parties and mowing the lawn and shopping for tile. Family. Bored even thinking about it.

It was the third inning. Van still had time. He waved to Ashley, who shuffled her feet out in left field. She waved back. Van walked out of the park and across the street to the 7-11. He closed his eyes and his skin looked blotchy and scratched. He bought a pack of cigs and stretched his quad. His knee killed him, so he opened the pack and lit his cigarette. A man in a ratty t-shirt and camouflage shorts leaned against the building. The sign around his neck said "Looking for work." Van handed him a dollar. He usually didn't give anything, but the guy looked like hell. Rough shape. He could be anybody.

He bet this guy didn't exactly have many friends either. He'd use that example later on Cheryl.

Van stamped out his cigarette and walked back to catch the end of Ashley's softball game. She must have wondered where he wandered off to.

He was on his slow way getting there. That's where he was.

38

When Ashley said she'd like to play softball, Cheryl said, "That sounds great—let's get you signed up." Van felt circumspect, asked his daughter if she really wanted to go that route. Perhaps athleticism was not really Ashley's strong suit? She felt the desire, but did she have the hand-eye? Tossing the ball around in the yard, she had difficulty. There was the time the ball caught her square on the nose, blood gurgling all over her green Gap t-shirt.

He knew he'd have to work with her.

Batting practice occupied most of March. He took her out to the middle school and pitched her old tennis balls.

"If you can hit those you can hit something larger," Van said. "So this is good practice."

She swung and missed again. Van did not wish she had been born a boy instead—he didn't. He did wish she possessed more natural ability though, some kind of inner fire that would propel her forward; some things cannot be taught. Fire is one of them.

Van sidled up to Ashley and tapped her left shoulder.

"This is the key, Ash. You have to keep this tucked. As the ball is coming toward you keep it tucked until the very last moment. Then let your hands and legs do the work."

He fed her balls for an hour and they played catch and he tossed her popups and ground balls.

He drove Ashley home, a smile on her face. That was the most important part, he reminded himself. She enjoyed it. She was plenty patient with the gnats and the weeds and the sticky humidity. She wanted to be a player. She wanted to please him.

However, when it came time to play for the team, the coach stuck her in the outfield. Most balls wouldn't reach her. The coach knew she was just a beginner with a lot of work to do to overcome this.

Van hated watching the games, with the exception of Ashley's at bats—the only moments when the action revolved around here. Invariably she struck out, but this made the slow advances that much more noticeable: even a foul ball was an occasion for small celebration.

But Van could not get past the elementary errors (especially mental). Nobody on either team seemed able to catch the ball. The coach behaved in a half-assed manner and emitted platitudes rather than offering actual softball knowledge. "Bend your knees. A walk is as good as a hit. Keep your eye on the ball." These statements meant nothing. A tall rangy guy who sported mossy facial scruff, the coach liked to say "Swing at something good," or "sharp hit, swing it good," or "frozen rope coming up." The girls did not seem to understand that one.

The games seemed extremely slow. Slow pitch. No stealing. The ball just floating there in the air and many girls still couldn't hit it. He wanted to jump into the fray and teach and demonstrate.

One afternoon, after Ashley's team lost, Van drove her to get a Slurpee. He usually reserved Slurpee purchases for games where she at least got a hit or caught a fly ball, but those were both difficult to come by.

They sat on the curb and Ashley sucked on the Slurpee straw.

"Are you sure you want to do this softball thing?" He tried to muffle her sense of disappointment.

"For me it's fun," she said. "Even if I'm not that good."

Fun. Van barely knew the meaning of that word. Nothing was fun—everything was high stakes.

Van watched the fireflies ping in the darkness. Lightning flashed in the distance. The sky groaned with thunder. A storm loomed, but Van didn't seem to be in a hurry. He rarely was.

37

The in-laws were fond of Van for some reason, but it often displayed itself as tough love. They put up with his sometimes morose personality. They funneled money into Cheryl's bank account to help out. Van did not want help or ask for a thing, but it was most certainly welcome as far as he was concerned. Not one to look a gift horse in the mouth. He didn't know what to say about it really. Instead, he pretended it didn't happen, knowing that it did.

But the advice. The never-ending stream of guidance.

Every other Sunday they drove over to Cheryl's parents' house for dinner. It was a comforting ritual but one marked by a certain tension.

Her parents offered unsolicited advice about how to best find a sense of direction. Her engineer father and math teacher mother could not relate to Van's mid-career dithering.

He told them many times. He was a ballplayer—that's what and who he was. When *that* ended his work life also ended, as far as he was concerned. *He* ended. He only knew how to do one thing. As a way to appease his wife he worked on a way to parlay his baseball career into something else. It was not easy. Cheryl's parents suggested he was being lazy. If he could transfer his prior abilities into something else he would, but he frankly did not see the angle. He wasn't trying to be indolent. He just possessed zero idea.

"It's not that I want to sleep all day and sit around twiddling my thumbs. Tell me what else to do."

Mark suggested returning to school—finding a trade. Since Van only possessed a high school education, what could he do? It is only through education that you can pull yourself from your bootstraps, Mark said. "You'll be a better man as a result."

Christina had a wide array of tips: the common theme simply being occupying oneself in a productive manner. For the sake of appearances, if nothing else. Become a dance instructor. Fun baseball clinics at the local park. Invest in vending machines. Become a taxidermist. Open a restaurant or bar (good idea, Van thought). Get a job at the textile store in the mall. Learn to play the harp. Sell cacti by the side of the road. Be creative. Do something. Something. *Anything*.

"What do you *do* with yourself as is? How do you occupy yourself?"

They ate veal cutlets with garlic mashed potatoes. Cheryl seemed to have an affinity for celebrity cookbooks.

"Well, you know how it is."

"No, not exactly. I'm curious."

"Josh comes home from school at three, so I help out with that. I do errands while Cheryl is at work. Odds and ends, you know."

Christina clicked her teeth and took quick sips from her water. Cheryl watched.

"Does that leave you fulfilled?"

"Mom," Cheryl said. "Let's give it a break for now."

"I'm sorry, I'm just wondering how things work."

Van said he's figuring things out. Said that it's a process. A work in progress. Aren't we all?

Cheryl's father changed the subject.

Josh and Ashley sat at their table. Josh ate carrot sticks and colored a picture of a sailboat in a coloring book. Ashley looked upset. She knew.

After dinner the family played games—that was the tradition. Cards usually—sometimes Scrabble or checkers or Trivial Pursuit.

This night they played Pictionary.

Christina brought out the brownies and ice cream. Van passed, knowing it would sting her.

"Are you full?"

"I am tonight," he said. "No room right now, so full."

"Suit yourself."

"I will, thanks," Van said. Inner smirk.

During the drive home Cheryl apologized for her mother's behavior, explaining that once she gets fixed on an idea it's difficult for her to let go.

"It's okay," Van said. "She just wants a good life for her grandchildren. There's nothing wrong with that."

Cheryl held his hand as he drove. It helped.

But clouds built within him. They scudded through borne on unseen westerlies.

36

Van was on pick-up duty, so he decided to make the best of it. Josh could be a surly four-year-old. He mirrored Van's sullenness. Josh too did not want to be touched or looked at or spoken to. If Van reached for him Josh swatted at his hand. He squirmed. This made Van's life difficult. Van wanted to be a good father, though he felt he couldn't be. Josh wouldn't let him.

Rain dribbled and spat. Josh sat in the back. Van plunked him in the safety seat, even though Josh said he hated it. He tugged at the straps and yanked himself free.

"How're you doing, kiddo?"

Josh stared at the back of the seat and refused to open his mouth. Slid his hands over his mouth so that the point might seem obvious.

"Are you cold?"

No answer.

"It's rainy. You want some soup when we get home?"

No answer.

Josh's nursery school teacher told Van and Cheryl that Josh had a different way about him. He did not like to share with the other boys.

Why does everything have to be a challenge?

Why can't one simple thing go right, go easy?

Van drove slowly, looking back at his son often.

He remembered the Wiffle balls and bat rattling about in the trunk. He wondered. It wasn't *that* rainy, he thought.

As Van approached the local park, he decided. He pulled off the road and into the park and pulled in front of the field next to the picnic pavilion and swing sets.

Van parked and loped around to Josh's side.

"Hey, buddy. Let's go get some exercise."

"No," Josh said. "I don't want to."

"We're going to play catch, hit some balls."

"No," Josh said.

Van tried to maneuver Josh out of his seat but Josh smacked his fists against the back of the seat, screamed, threw a fit, saying that he felt hungry and didn't want to play. But Van pulled him out anyway. Josh bawled continuously and for a moment Van loathed his son—hated the stubborn, stupid will in him.

Josh stood in the middle of the wet field, rain drifting all around. Van handed him a bat and tossed him a ball, but by the time it slowly arced its way to Josh, he had already turned away from his father and started whacking weeds at the base of the dogwood.

"Josh, I'm going to toss you some balls. You want to see if you can hit them?"

Josh said nothing. He thwacked the weeds all around, swinging wildly.

That night Van told Cheryl of his frustrations. She listened with one hand on her chin.

"There's something about him," Van said. "He bristles. His drive is too strong, too certain for no good reason."

"You know how they go through phases. He's only four, you know."

Van worried though. Once a pattern is set it can be difficult to undo. Cheryl knew this better than anyone. Van felt she tried to mollify him, to brush his concerns under the rug.

"He doesn't seem to want a relationship with me," Van said. He felt faintly ridiculous just saying it. But it seemed true.

He closed his eyes and listened to the crickets. They sounded piercing that night. The woods, not far off. His mind slipped there.

35

Van's parents wanted a family vacation, like the old days. The three of them sprawled on an island—somewhere in the Caribbean. Somewhere a bit fancier than they could afford.

"We can all afford it *now*," Van's dad said. "Why not?"

But Van demurred. He had kids—he'd have to bring everybody along. Not only would that add up but it would not necessarily be that appealing.

90

"Cheryl can't do without you for a few days?" His mother frequently defended him.

"Of course she can," Van said. "But there will be a price to pay."

"I'm concerned," she said.

"Don't be concerned. Everything is fine. Don't worry."

"You just can't pull yourself away for a few days."

"Let's come up with another option."

Van's mother suggested a day trip. They could drive out to the mountains, do some hiking, and snag a bite to eat on the way back. It wouldn't be the Caribbean, but it would be nice.

"Can Cheryl do without you for a day? If you like I can call her to stress the importance...."

"Yes, that should be fine."

Van felt the strain. Nothing unique to him, he knew; in fact the weariness seemed all too familiar—something from the movies. Everyone fell into patterns not of their design.

So they went. Van's father drove and the fall day was brisk and windy and spirited. They ate granola bars in the car and drank seltzer and the sun slanted through the windshield. Van could see to the horizon. He stretched his eyes.

They hiked several hours up to the top of the ridge and stopped to eat apples and drink water and soak in the view. Van knew his father went along for the ride on this. He didn't exactly complain, but Van knew where he wanted to be. His father winked at him, but Van averted his eyes. He hated the winking; he knew what *that* meant.

Van felt energetic. His mother was right to press for a change of pace. His knee even felt a bit better—mind over matter? Who knows? Good days, bad days. Maybe he could still strengthen?

They hiked down the ridge and up another. Van watched the leaves swirl above and land around them. His legs felt the burning. It was good.

91

"This land has been here forever," his mother said. "It will still be here when we're all gone. All of us. Isn't that something to think about?"

"It's a hard fact," Van's father said. "Also depressing."

Van watched them.

"We have something to tell you," Van's mother said.

They sat on a lichen covered rock. They told him that their estate would go to Van's uncle when they died—his father's brother. "He owns practically nothing and he had a tough life," Van's father said. "You made something good out of yours and you don't need us as much. That's the difference. We're not worried about your future."

But maybe they should be? How could they be so sure? A weight dropped in Van's stomach, a kind of dread.

"That's your decision," Van said. It felt abstract, like a world away. It barely registered.

"We love you and want to make sure you understand," Van's mother said. "It's not a personal thing. We just wanted to say it so you know now. That's all."

Van watched his father. He couldn't tell if he winked at him again or if some dust made its way into his eyes.

They ate at Josie's Grill on the way back. The hamburger tasted especially juicy. Van let the juices linger in his mouth for just a moment longer. Even the iced tea seemed even more refreshing than it usually did. He drank it down. His parents paid the tab and drove home. Van in the back.

34

Cheryl wanted to go fishing without the kids. So they dropped Ashley and Josh off at her parents' house. It was a thick, soggy July morning.

Van didn't know why fishing—she had never really expressed an interest before.

He didn't ask.

They bought worms and drove to the reservoir. The reservoir lay near the dump (they passed it on the way). It was quiet there, usually, so Van looked forward to going. He craved a cigarette, but Cheryl would give him ten kinds of hell if he smoked even one. He almost felt a hankering for a beer, but not quite. Not a distinct desire, more like a misty wish from another life.

Their rods seemed old and creaky—Van barely used them anymore—they showed their age from disuse. But once Van cleaned them up, they functioned. With his pocket knife Van sliced a worm in half and baited the rods.

"You remember how to cast?"

Cheryl rolled her eyes. He knew she fished a lot as a girl, a fact that came up early on in their courtship.

Van held a thermos filled with diluted apple juice and ice. Cheryl packed peanut butter sandwiches and quartered Granny Smiths. Slight brown edges.

They crept along the shore, close to the bridge. Sparse, empty. Nobody sat under the bridge, which Van liked. They could make their way down there later if they struck out in the tree shadows.

Van and Cheryl sat on the shore and cast and recast. They sat in silence for a long time, watching. Van felt a few nibbles—or maybe they were snags. But they didn't catch anything. Cheryl barely even got a nibble.

So they tried under the bridge.

They stood on the concrete base and dangled their lines down into the water. It smelled dank and muddy and the echoes reverberated.

"Are you happy?" Cheryl didn't look at him. She asked it and stared down into the water, as if an eel or catfish would bring back the answer through the murk.

"Yeah, life is good," Van said. He didn't mean it 100%. He knew that. But was there ever a 100%?

"Are you sure? You seem maybe just a bit out of whack. The kids, the house. I'm not sure. None of it is new now. You're still happy?"

Van hated when she went full-bore analytical on him, attempting to sniff out some potential drama. He was not fond of being inspected by anyone, especially someone who knew him so well.

Cheryl almost displayed a need for conflict.

No good answer to her question—the worst part.

"I wouldn't be here if it wasn't what I wanted," he said.

"That same bullshit," Cheryl said. "You'd go along just fine. You'd glide with it."

Van reeled in.

"You wanted to go fishing to ask me if I'm okay?"

"No," Cheryl said. "It just popped into my head. I wonder all the time though—you know that. I guess I should relax, but I can't. My parents pop into my head, also. Lots of things do. You know me by now, I hope."

Van wished something would bite—a much needed distraction.

"What if I said no?"

"Then we'd have to do something. We'd have to make a change. What's the point of it all if we're not where we want to be?"

Van was pissed. On this occasion, Cheryl came at him with an abstraction, some convoluted nonsense about his inner self.

He was fine and even if he wasn't, he could adjust. That's part of life—finding your way around—the worst. But also, everything felt fine. He was never the best father and he still had no clue how to effectively provide for his family, but he felt fine. Wasn't that enough? The internal compass.

33

Jesus died at 33. Not an auspicious year numerologically, Van thought. He felt a storm cloud hovering over him. When he peered up in the sky, rain inevitably lurked on the horizon. Yet, his windshield wipers never seemed to fully operate. Instead, they smeared.

If only Van had a better sense of humor, that would help him. He was never a funny guy, at least never thought himself as such. And when he did try to make light of a situation it usually backfired. He didn't even know any jokes.

Van had only been married three years but it already felt like thirty. His life somehow seemed ever-so slightly stale. He held Josh and didn't know what to say or do. So he bobbed the little guy in his arms and felt awkward and ineffectual. He did this for five minutes, then passed the bundle back to Cheryl. She was the mother; she knew how to keep the boy entertained.

When Ashley was just one she, of course, lacked a personality also, but at three Van felt a greater sense of interest. He could *talk* to her. She could listen. They could do things together. Van told himself not to think about where his career would be if he still played. It wasn't productive or helpful. Not *constructive*. This kind of thinking just lead him down a rabbit hole. That could only exist in another universe.

Still, he couldn't help reading the box scores. He couldn't help noticing his teammates—ex-teammates—still producing, still going at it. Elly batted .307—that had to raise his lifetime average a few clicks. Jumbo had nine wins under his belt already that year—good for him. Chad hit eighteen dingers and forty-seven RBIS—he would produce a monster year. He rooted for those guys, and they still had a winning team. Just not quite as good. Wished he was a broadcaster, still connected to the game somehow.

At dinner he ran out of things to talk about, or that's how he felt. Van was not the most naturally outgoing sort, or anything remotely close, really. They mostly talked about the kids—how Ashley needed more clothes ("she keeps growing and growing"), how Josh really seemed alert, *despite* his nap. *Amazing.* Cheryl was likely tired from work, Van thought. Van had little reason to be tired. He did call the club to check in on their medical coverage now that he was retired. He double-checked his pension. Good there. Not a lot, but enough to see him through.

Van dreaded the first few minutes after Cheryl put the kids to bed. This is when the staleness became most obvious. He had little to say, and she seemed to lack interest in speaking to him or asking him pertinent questions. They usually retired to the living room and turned on the television. Van fell asleep on the couch by 10:00 p.m. Cheryl read a magazine. It was as if they lived in a doctor's waiting room. But what were they waiting *for*? They were waiting for something.

"There's a good article about the best way to power wash the deck," Cheryl said.

Van nodded, drifted off.

He imagined trees above him, the wind through the wild flowers on the bank of a muddy river.

"Mmmm," he said. "That's interesting."

"We should do that. It's been a few years."

"Yeah," Van said. "Good idea."

He rarely thought about curveballs. He rarely thought about lacing up his spikes. He did not think about the warning track, or the thick smell of cigar smoke wafting from the stands, or the music thumping through the center field speakers, or the glove of some woman's white tank top or the red seams hissing in the air.

"Do you want me to make some brownies tomorrow? That might go well with ice cream. Have a quart of vanilla already."

"Sure," Van said. "That would be good."

"I'll mow the grass tomorrow."

"Great, it's getting pretty long."

Van never thought about the patterns in the grass, or the chalk, or the sound of the umpire's clicker, or the ball popping into the glove, or the crack of the Louisville Slugger, the arc of the ball dipping over the second baseman's head, falling in safely into the crisscrossed grass. He rarely thought about the potential hits he could be hitting or the diving shoestring catches he could make or the throws from the warning track all the way to third on the fly, just ahead of the runner.

What was the point of it all? Who was he now? Where was he going?

32

On the day his son was born Van underwent his fourth knee surgery.

"While you have me under, just go ahead and slit my throat," Van told the surgeon. He meant it as a caustic statement. The surgeon's eyes widened. He couldn't be unfamiliar with the despair which someone in Van's position must have felt. And yet he didn't laugh or smile at the gallows humor.

"Just some housecleaning," the surgeon said.

When he came out of the surgery, Van vomited. Like clockwork. The anesthetic got him. He knew he would. The nurse informed him that his wife was going into labor. She wheeled him to the delivery room and he watched.

"Cheryl, I'm here with you," he said.

She couldn't respond through her wailing screams.

When he heard the infant's cry he knew it would be a boy. Somehow he knew.

"It's a boy," the nurse told him.

"Joshua," Van said. "My son."

He had already doubled the number of children his parents raised. His children would not grow up as an island as he did. They would have each other: a brother and a sister. A tandem. Always someone to look after you.

Ashley acted jealous, even at two. He could see it in her eyes. She would get used to it—begin to see how having a brother could be advantageous in many ways, but it would take time.

For several weeks Van hobbled on crutches. Crutches began to feel natural to Van.

He made love with his wife often when Josh was young. Something about the birth of his son, about being laid-up. Something about her profound luxuriance, the way her body returned to itself.

He loved her, and despite his knee he still felt young. He was in the prime of his life. Life was good. He could get used to the parent thing, he thought. I can do it, he thought. It's just another skill to master.

The knee brace helped him get around. Without that he wouldn't have even been able to do all the work he did. Even though they had resided in the house for a couple of years, much still needed to be done. He didn't mind doing it: working with his hands kept his mind occupied, pulled him away from thoughts of his career, his broken body.

The main project: finishing the basement. Nothing unusual in this. They agreed that the basement should be a place for the children to play in the winter, on a rainy day. It needed carpeting. He needed to remove the bar and patch the dry wall in a few spots. Also, some electrical work—dark down there. Also, Van needed to install a sump pump. Flooding was a problem in years past, presumably. Also, he needed to dig a drainage ditch.

Van hired two young men—teenagers who lived in the neighborhood: Phil and Kelvin. Phil was an honor student, or so he claimed, and he bragged about cutting his teeth on neighborhood lawn mowing and mulching. His father taught him a few things about home repair and as long as Van could direct him Phil said he could be a help. Kelvin lived across the street—the son of Mitch and Maggie—Cheryl was fond of them both. Kelvin was younger, but strong and he played linebacker for his high school. Extra walking around money for him.

They played the Rolling Stones and Grateful Dead, and got the job done. It took two months and Van made mistakes (incorrectly wired the lighting in the front part of the room and then had to redo the whole thing; the laborious dry wall, and Van bought too much material in the

98

first place). The kids just went along for the ride. Van liked having them around—it reminded him of being on a team again. Their youth rubbed off on him and as a result he felt younger, vicariously. Even if he couldn't walk very well, he felt their energy.

Van didn't even mind that Kelvin stared a bit too long at his wife. He knew Kelvin watched her through his binoculars. It didn't bother him (maybe it should have). As long as Kelvin helped with the basement and kept his hands to himself and his tongue in his mouth.

"We're done now," Van said one evening. Cheryl had just returned from work—her first month back after maternity leave.

"That's great. Let me take a look."

She seemed excited. She seemed pleased. They made love in the basement that night. Christened it, she said.

"Those kids were good, weren't they?"

"Yeah, they helped out," Van said.

Cheryl nodded. Van wondered if she knew about the binoculars. She probably did, he surmised. Not everything needed to be known. Just most things.

"Do you like having me home now?"

"I do," Cheryl said. "Have to admit."

31

For one year and one year only Van tried to coach baseball. Westmark High School seemed desperate for someone, anyone, and knew of him through local newspapers and word of mouth (everyone seemed to know, in theory, that a big leaguer, a former champion, existed in their midst). The old coach needed to leave the area suddenly—his father died, and his infirm mother needed his help in Upstate New York. A last-minute thing.

Van agreed, on the condition that his assistant coach deal with parental concerns. He felt too young (and emotionally fragile) to confront additional vicarious egos. Westmark agreed. He would be paid $2,600 for the season, pre-tax. It was nothing, but at least it would keep him busy and connected to the game some, also.

The team showed initial promise. Consisting mostly of juniors and sophomores, with a smattering of freshmen, they seemed enthusiastic and played with energetic verve. They loved to practice. They loved to laugh and goof around.

But the fundamentals. But the mental game.

Joey possessed hands of iron on first—frustrating to the other infielders, who were mostly adept and could throw. The catcher made poor decisions and had a rag arm as a result of injuries. The opposing teams stole on him with ease. The outfielders seemed generally slow or slightly uncoordinated. But worst of all, the pitchers walked far too many batters. A typical game involved a freebie an inning, sometimes more. Difficult to win that way. They only won two games out of their sixteen-game schedule, and both were over teams completely depleted by injuries.

It was an odd time in Van's life. He liked being involved; the problem was that he wasn't involved, not *fully*. He wanted to pick up a glove and show them how it worked. He wanted to hit for them, run for them. Think for them. Make decisions for them. Play for them. He felt transitional, but into what?

The team could hit, but it was sporadic. Vick and Jim and Calvin had wheels, but the other weaknesses glared. Nick and Bryan, the best hitters on the squad, couldn't field or pitch. Billy and Matt possessed all the right tools but could easily sink into a mentally unfocused state. All of these kids were all fifteen and sixteen—sophomores, juniors. Few seniors, for whatever reason. Most of the team couldn't even drive themselves to practice.

Mike Baylor was nice enough to assist, which did help considerably. He was unable to provide a complete buffer from the parents—an impossibility—but he acted as a filter, which gave Van time and energy to focus on X's and O's. He answered questions, took calls, made calls.

Mostly the Hawks lost 11-3, 12-4. The games weren't close; and they were ugly. By the third inning the writing usually was scrawled on the wall. At times Van needed to excuse himself, disappear into the shrubbery for a moment of quiet reflection.

Van didn't scream. He didn't shout. He offered many firm talks, but mostly he was content to let the players play. They understood their mistakes on some basic level. It took some doing to underscore the importance of the mental component of the game. Difference between winning and losing.

Usually Van actively dissuaded Cheryl from attending. Bad enough losing in front of the birds and squirrels.

"It's not going to be fun for you to watch these kids. They're still learning. It's still pretty basic." She shrugged; more time for her to do her thing.

At the conclusion of the season Van's players (and their parents) threw him a thank you party at the local pizza joint. They bought him beer and gave him a trophy which read "Coach of the Year." He was moved.

At the beginning of the next week Van tendered his resignation. In his letter he thanked the school for the opportunity, but stated that he wanted "more time with his children."

Several parents called him at home to try to persuade him to come back. "We need your guidance; you're great with those kids." But Van was all set. Maybe in another lifetime.

30

Who *are* these people? There was a girl in a crib in a room down the hall. A woman reclined in bed next to him claiming she was his wife. There was a large house in the suburbs. He received a hefty paycheck every other week, though he hadn't worked in two years. There was a sense of unreality. There was a sense that he was playing at adulthood, but not fully participating in it. Whose life was this? Whose house?

101

On some level Van felt out of his element, over his head in complications. Not that he had a problem with Cheryl, much less this little girl for whom he, it seemed, was half-responsible. He simply didn't *know* them. Who was he married to? At one moment she was just another groupie at an autograph session, the next thing he knew they owned a house together. Then they had a family. His head reeled. Van felt ambushed by his own life, by his own decisions. Was he complacent? Did he make a mistake, choosing pleasure over sensibility? He lost his sense of balance and proportion.

The house largely sat unfurnished, many rooms empty, bare. Now that Ashley was a reality and the high drama of his relationship with Cheryl came to a completion, they would fill out their lives. The empty rooms didn't particularly bother him. He would leave the domesticity up to her. She cared about such things. As far as he was concerned, they could furnish the house with milk crates.

They decided Van would take care of Ashley when Cheryl returned to work. She didn't have to work; she wanted to. Van found caring for his daughter relaxing on some level. She *cooed* at him. He gazed into her eyes—and they looked like *his* eyes. He accepted her rhythms—her crying; her need for formula; her need for sleep; her need to be changed. During the day it was his daughter, and he watched from the sidelines. Then Cheryl returned home. He wasn't always sure what to say to her. Sometimes he stood there dumbfounded.

"How was your day?" She sat on the other side of the table. Ashley lay asleep upstairs.

"It was fine. It was a good day," he said. "And how about work?"

"Good. Busy, but good. Not bad."

"Great."

"Good, yeah great."

He knifed into his potato, watching steam seep from it. He plopped an ovoid glob of sour cream onto it and spread it around the potato with his fork. He had no idea what to say to Cheryl. What was he supposed to *talk* about? What were they supposed to *do*? Was he supposed to go through this pantomime for the rest of his life?

Cheryl smiled at him and bent her neck down into her plate. Her cheeks flushed. She took a sip from her chardonnay. She possessed remarkable high cheek bones, as if God sculpted her face from marble. Even Cheryl must have know she looked quite stunning—anyone with functioning eyes could see that.

"I was thinking," she said. "It might be nice if we had some help."

"What do you mean?" She already wanted therapy? He worried.

"The conversations. Maybe some starters? They have books of topics. It's not an unusual problem, is it?"

Van thought, what's the harm?

So Cheryl bought a book of topics and subtopics and conversational starters. The book was entitled *Get Talking*. Many topics leaned into an abstract or hypothetical bent. What would you do if your father said he once killed a man? Where would you reside if you had only one month left to live? Discuss your favorite childhood memories revolving around the opposite sex.

Instead of dreading dinner, Van looked forward to the subtopic. What would they talk about *that* evening? He made it a project.

But after several weeks, his interest waned and he began to view the book as quietly demeaning to their relationship. The conversation points felt like cocktail party banter, artificial—something to talk about because you had nothing to talk about.

"Let's just talk about, you know, normal things," he said. "Whatever comes to our minds first. How does that sound?"

"Okay," Cheryl said. She drank her merlot and smiled. "Whatever you want is fine.

Cheryl was so good-natured, so understanding. She was aglow still. Van should honor this, he thought. He should savor it, make it last.

They sat in silence. They watched old TV shows. Van ran through a series of topics in his head: religion, science, nature, dreams, aliens, politics. All too broad, too energy-sucking. He thought better of each topic.

Instead, Van cut into his green beans. He watched Cheryl do the same—a mirror of him. Their utensils clinked against their plates, one at a time. Van noticed the reverberation.

29

A new shoe store opened at the mall. Slim and Freddy wanted to skip the autograph session and hit the waterski shack on the bay instead.

"Call it a family emergency," Slim said. "We don't owe these people nothing." Freddy just wanted beer and women—in that order; he didn't care where they went.

"Why don't we go waterskiing after?" Van said. "I could use the dough." He tapped his knee. He knew his pay checks would stop one day in the not-too-distant future. Then what? Might as well cash in while people still remembered his name and what he did. That wouldn't last long. Good Karma, also.

"Alright, man. Anything for you," Slim said.

"But you owe us both a beer. Make it two."

They sat at the table in front of the shoe store. Kids bounded up to them with baseballs and hats and photos and the players signed them quickly and gave them high fives. The adults carried programs and old baseball cards or team balls. Some held scraps of paper or index cards. Some dangled baseball caps or pennants.

Van usually didn't look up—just signed. But she stood in front of him—huge blue eyes and hair and body and she told Van he was her favorite player ever. *Ever*, she said. "Want to hear something, a secret?" She lowered her voice. "I think you're *soulful*, like you've lost something. Like you left something behind. I can see it all, it's in your eyes. I *know* you on some level."

"What's your name?"

"Cheryl," she said. "What's yours? Oh, never mind. I'm so nervous. I know you and I watch you all the time, of course. Still, I'm so nervous. I've been meaning to meet you for so long. And now here you are. I know you are Van Boyle. I know your lifetime batting average is .268. I know you won at least two gold gloves—but it should have been way more. You have class. You're my favorite. Ever."

He looked up.

Freddy turned his head toward them, eavesdropping.

"Two—that's right."

"Would you like to go out on the lake with us?" Freddy asked. "Waterskiing."

He surprised Van, that was for sure.

And they drove down to the bay where the boat ran fast. Van sat in back and watched the water leap and lap and spray as Cheryl hung on, laughing.

"I've never done this," she roared, laughing. They made her year, her life. "I don't do *this*."

Van couldn't help watching her, mesmerized. She looked like perfection, beauty incarnate. He knew nothing about her, but everything changed at this moment. It was as if a switch clicked from left to right. And it stuck. He wanted her. He desired her. At that moment she was everything and all. The bees knees and all the other parts, too.

And then she fell into the water.

"She's down," Van shouted. "She fell!"

"Don't worry, man," Freddy said. "She'll be fine. It's just water. You're *supposed* to fall in it."

And the boat slowed and swung around in a loop and idled next to her. She grasped Van's hand and he pulled her up into the boat and she hugged him, wet and laughing, a smile spreading wide—from ear to ear.

"That *was* something," she said.

"Yes, it sure was," Van said. Slim eyeballed him. His turn.

105

"Don't laugh at me," he said.

"I won't," Van said. He knew he wouldn't even watch. His attention lay somewhere else.

Cheryl sat next to him, dripping wet.

"I do have a towel," Van said, and he dried her. Her hair dripped a puddle at his feet and he let his feet shuffle into it.

She saw the movement.

He saw her eyes watching him.

The water never seemed clearer. The beat bumped faster, charging ahead.

He watched her eyes watching him.

The water never seemed clearer, more infused with light. The boat was fast and it zipped ahead. The spray fountained into the sun.

28

Van never liked doctors. Never *trusted* them.

Even the surgeons—yes, they correctly asserted that his knee would never be the same again, but why shouldn't he push it? Why shouldn't he at least make an effort? Was he supposed to simply *give up*, throw in the towel? Yes, he only had one good knee left, but he also only had one *career*. One time to shine.

The third surgery went well and after three months he felt fine. Bud said, "No way, Jose. Not now, maybe after another three months. Two months and then a rehab assignment in Rochester—maybe. Listen to your *body*." Bud sounded just like the doctors; they had colluded in their effort to end his career—Bud simply acted as their mouthpiece. Van felt jinxed; he knew he was jinxed.

It's just a knee, Van thought. Mind over matter—he can overcome it. Pain is all between the ears, so the saying goes.

But then, he realized, it's not. It's more comprehensive. It spreads. Becomes its own reality.

After weeks of strengthening, light jogging, stretching, he tried the rehab assignment. It was late July and even in Rochester, New York, it boiled at ninety-five just about every day. They stuck him in left field, as in the outfield it might be less likely to need an all-out sprint. But even there it was difficult. He lacked the ability to push off. That first step was a lightning bolt through his quad, deep into the knee. With each pounding step it felt as if a long screw jabbed into him.

Batting was, if anything, worse. He slapped at the ball, that's all he could do. Van couldn't thrust *into* it. No legs. No hips. As a result, he lacked power—no push off. Frustrating as hell.

A week in he felt little progress at all. The team doc said he had to be patient. He had to let his body heal. His body went through a trauma, and he had to accept that—accept the limitations for now.

Van didn't want to hear about limitations.

Bud extended the rehab assignment—two weeks, then three weeks, then a month. After a month Bud gave Van a call.

"How are you feeling, champ?"

"Let's give it a go."

"You didn't answer my question."

"I'm feeling okay. Okay is okay."

"That's not what I hoped to hear."

But Bud gave in, said that Van could rejoin the team if the doc said so. Doctor Williams did, cautiously. He wondered what ever happened to Kelly. He wondered that often.

"It's not ideal. But you have made progress. You have improved."

Van was in the starting lineup two days later starting in center field. Before the game he stared at the wall, cursing it. He couldn't believe an inanimate object altered his career so drastically—a slab of vertical concrete with padding—that's all it was. Why couldn't they have made it out of cardboard? Then he'd have a knee, he'd have a career, he'd have his life.

The first game—no problem. He struck out three times and popped out once. Seeing the ball spiraling up into the air, he sprinted from the batter's box but then immediately slowed. Van almost wondered if some part of his unconscious mind protected himself, avoiding the exertion.

In the field he caught two easy flies and another rain maker, which he almost lost in the lights. He was able to play several singles in front of him, toss the ball back to second. There was one gapper, but he couldn't reach it, so Eddie Floyd picked it up off the ricochet, instead.

Van was glad he *survived*. He lived to play another day. Even if he was slow and ineffective.

But during the second game back Van bolted deep to catch a drive. He ran as fast as his wheels would take him, ignoring the pain in his knee. He dove to catch the ball and landed square on the injured knee. The ball bounced away from him, but Van felt unable to move. It was as if his body took over. He felt paralyzed.

The trainer and Eddie helped him off the field. Three days later he needed to have another operation. That's it, Van thought. I'm toast.

He announced his retirement from baseball the next Friday.

27

Van had a great year—perhaps the best of his career. In April he hit .327, blasting drives all over the field—even his outs were frozen ropes. He felt relaxed, seeing the ball well. It looked like a watermelon. A cantaloupe. A white ball just waiting to be smacked. His hands felt lightning quick. He didn't commit a single error and threw out several base-runners at second. The series against the Yankees was one of his best ever—when he hit three dingers and drove in seven. Even Van was surprised by his power.

May was even stronger, in some respects. That month the O's played a slew of home games and Van started the vast majority. He hit .335—stole bases, scored runs. The O's were playing great ball and Van felt good just to be alive. He made a few throwing errors in the White Sox series, but otherwise Van felt excited. Even the errors he could explain. He knew he just over-extended himself, tried a bit *too hard*.

After the games Van hit the town. Usually this included Freddy and Slim, sometimes Eddie. Carl came along when he could. They frequently invited Bud, but as the manager, he couldn't. He didn't want to compromise his authority.

"What authority?" Slim joked.

"I don't want any Babe Ruths, now," Bud said.

He didn't mean it as a compliment. Bud called Ruth "the drunken Indian."

The availability of women astounded him. Cindy called him "the stud" and Vickie said he was like Don Juan with a bat.

"Talk softly and carry a big stick," he said. "Do you like my big stick?"

"Who said that?" Amber said. He liked them with too much mascara. He liked them with stilettos and tight clothing.

"I did. I made it up," Van said.

"You so did not!"

"But I almost had you," Van said.

"Mmmm, come *here*," Amber said.

The women weren't a distraction to him, as much as they were to other guys. If Eddie met a woman the night before, the joke stood that he'd strike out three times the next day. Van enjoyed his life and he rarely if ever thought of anything beyond the moment. Especially if it was a day game. Marriage and kids were a distant mirage, if that.

Van blamed it on the booze as much as the ladies—but Eddie refused to listen to teetotaler Van. What did *he* know?

Van felt zero pressure to do anything in particular. He didn't have to settle down. He didn't have to be anywhere. He could relax and enjoy the bounty of life. He could have two at once if he wanted, and he did, especially if he had a big night at the plate. He could order caviar and let it sit there, untouched. He did. He could pour champagne in the bathtub and let one of the ladies take a bath in it. And he did. He could run naked through the hotel corridor, so he did that also.

Amber was his favorite, if he had to pick one. She was Greek and her skin glowed and he loved the way her mouth bowed and released. There was something about her pointy nipples and the tiny banana-shaped mole just above her left breast. She had a sweet, swaying disposition. They played cards after sex and talked about nightmares and ridiculous relatives.

They lounged, Amber smoking a joint with curlicued lips.

"What do you want to *do*?" she asked.

The sheets and covers slithered from the bed to the floor.

"I did all the doing I'm going to do," Van said. "I mean, wow."

Amber's father owned a diner. She worked as waitress in it.

"You know, I lied to you—I don't even really like baseball," she said. "I just like the fact that you're on television. I can watch you when you don't even know it. Baseball—it's a little *slow* sometimes."

Van said he couldn't care less if she liked the sport or not.

"When the game's over, I don't think about it. I'm not obsessed with it or anything."

Amber tried to give Van a toke but Van waved her off.

"C'mon, once?"

"Nah," Van said. "I don't think so."

"I'm coming to the game next week. I can't wait."

That was the day. Early June they played the Tigers and Brown hit a long drive over his head. I'm going to chase that down, Van said and he ran as fast as he could. He could see the ball spinning away from him. He could see the rainbow arc. And he ran to where he thought the rainbow would land. The sun blasted his face. His legs churned; his spikes dug into the grass.

But as he reached out about to catch the ball his body slammed into the wall, right knee first.

He could feel it crack and fold into itself. It *crumpled*. It caved-in. It *collapsed*.

Van vaguely remembers the stretcher. He vaguely recalls Bud leaning over him. He could smell Bud's distinct, leathery aftershave.

"You'll be okay, kiddo. It's just a bone bruise. We'll get you back in no time."

Van believed it. He thought it could be minor. Something he could overcome. It's not going to be an issue, he thought. A couple days off, he'd be back to normal.

26

Van's parents rarely came to watch Van play, but when they did Van always played nervously. He figured his lifetime batting average with his parents in the stands stood at sub-.200. He felt the eyes. He felt the need to impress.

Unfortunately, Van's parents watched from the stands in early May when Van found himself mired in a deep slump—offensively and out in center, also. His confidence dissolved. He felt mentally piss-poor and slow and awkward and he swung at balls way outside of the hitting zone. He made errors on basic decisions.

Bud put Van on a platoon with Gregg Bongert. The O's picked him up in a trade with Philadelphia. Bongert was young and speedy and played balls-to-the-wall on everything: a slap hitter with a way of annoying pitchers with his ability to serve the ball through the hole between first and second.

Then he rattled them on the bases.

Bud liked Bongert's moxie.

By early June Bongert was hitting .290 and Van hovered around .245. Van's power numbers seemed better, but Bongert was less error-prone in the field and showed more grit and hustle.

Van felt his stomach drop.

Also, Van didn't like Gregg. Gregg lacked "people skills," as Slim put it. He kept to himself and frequently made odd comments. He came across as egotistic and hot-headed.

"You have long legs," Gregg said once.

"What do you mean?"

"It's like your legs are too long for your body."

Gregg said this right before Van was set to hit. In the at bat Van hit a weak dribbler to the second baseman. Fucking Gregg, he thought. What does he mean I have *long* legs? What kind of asinine comment is that?

Another time Gregg told Van that he had a dream in which Van died in a motorcycle crash. And then vultures swooped down and carried off his arms. Another time Gregg told Van that his head looked just like a baseball, minus the seams. What did that mean? Was it a threat? An accusation?

Why would he tell me these things? Van thought Gregg was trying to get under his skin. His way of competing for the job. Gamesmanship at its worst.

Van asked for a sit-down with Bud.

A blistering day in early June. One of the first really hot days of the summer. Bud's office fan blew dusty air around the stuffy room.

"I know what you're going to say," Bud said. "But Gregg is playing well."

"That's not it," Van said. Van said he's a team player and if Bud feels Bongert is playing better, he should play him. "He's odd. The shit that comes out of his mouth. Can you ask him to stop saying things without thinking about them first? He needs a self-edit."

"You want me to *talk* to him about manners, is that what you're asking me? Don't we have games to win?"

"It's distracting me. *He's* distracting me."

Bud shrugged. I'll see what I can do, he said. Van couldn't be sure that he meant it. Bud, as always, cultivated a sense of mystery.

112

Van fantasized about pushing Gregg from an airplane, kicking him off a cliff.

It was a comfort to him.

The reality: he had to share time and he had to deal with or ignore Gregg's problem personality.

Then July happened. Gregg slipped into a tailspin, going 0-38 and Bud, as a result, sat him. Van would've thought Gregg would, as a result, clam it out of humility, but he talked even more. He began commenting on how sloppy the players looked in their uniforms, giving guys advice about how to best chew sunflower seeds, or how often to drink water to best maintain concentration. What the exact temperature water should be at ingestion.

Phil Perry didn't put up with it.

"What do you know? You haven't hit a solid ball since Easter," he snapped. You have the hand-eye coordination of a barrel of bricks.

Bud must've spoken to him, because suddenly Gregg stopped. He sulked in the clubhouse and only appeared in the dugout sporadically.

Van attained his position as the starting centerfielder again, which energized him. He started hitting again, upwards of .280 and he contributed to wins. He made plays in the field, stealing a few bases, walking. He did what Bongert was doing, only better.

By early August, management traded Bongert to Cincinnati—they needed another outfielder.

That night Van returned to his place and celebrated. Cigs and an apple pie. He hired a girl from down the Block to join him later. But first he ate several slices of pie, washing them down with water—cold enough to keep him energized.

Bongert, he thought. Fucking Bongert.

I always liked Gil Andrews, even though he pitched for the Indians. Andrews had a friendly rapport with everybody. During BP he'd seek out guys and joke around and hit some pepper and enjoy his life. He displayed the right attitude. He smiled constantly. Lots of banter. Lots of laughter.

During the game I couldn't touch him. Andrews pitched with movement on every ball. His curve ball started at my shoulders and dipped across the plate at my kneecaps. His slider angled like a diving eagle. His changeup seemed to stop mid-air and spin backwards away from me, and then it would fall off a cliff. And his rocket fastball zipped (with spin) to the corners of the plate. I could barely foul his pitches back.

I struck out four times, the golden sombrero.

But I sought him out after the game and told him he pitched great. Our whole team had difficulties against him. This guy.

"You want to get a bite?"

"Sure," he said.

So we went to this deli down off Pratt and ordered sandwiches. It was suppertime, but it was fine.

"How do you do it, man? You're so *loose* out there. I didn't have a clue. I didn't have a chance."

"I have no idea. It's just *instinct*, I guess. A lot of this is instinct. If I don't care about winning or losing, I do better. I just try to throw the ball. I don't know how else to describe it. I don't think too much."

"That's really something. I'm always tense up there, you know. Like I'm on edge. Trying too hard is what Bud says."

"That's me most of the time. Yeah, I'm on the opposition, so I shouldn't be giving you advice. But just relax up there and swing the bat. That's all it is. See ball, hit ball. People make things too complicated sometimes, get in their own way."

I was friends with Gil for years after that. We kept in touch for a long time.

After he retired he drowned in the Atlantic Ocean playing with his son. He strayed a bit too far out, caught in a riptide. And that was it. His son watched him sink into the pounding waves, into the froth.

25

Van was hyper-competitive. Van was even competitive about competition, believing he was more competitive than others who even dared to *think* they were competitive. When he lost, he wanted to *die*. Everyone on the team hated losing, but Van hated losing even more. Van hated losing so much he couldn't bring himself to utter the word "lose." He could be eccentric in his own way.

And yet at age twenty-five, the team lost. Bud claimed it had to do with fundamentals, but Van blamed chemistry and bad luck. Bud, like many baseball players, was superstitious. In July when the team sat ten games under .500 he dumped his girlfriend, cut his scraggly hair short, threw away all of his underwear and socks and bought new ones, gave all of his Mizuno bats away and switched to Louisville Sluggers, gave away all his batting gloves and got new ones, wore a different hat, ate at different restaurants, drank tea instead of coffee, brushed his teeth from left to right instead of right to left, slept on the *other* side of the bed with the lights on. Everything different.

The winning percentage did not increase.

A month later Van changed everything again. Losing was a *disease* and he wanted to extract it, pronto. But the more he tried, the worse he did. Van felt crappy all the time—about himself, about his life. He had no desire talk to anybody or play cards or go out. He wasn't that interested in women.

His ex-girlfriend called him all the time, saying she missed him. He never called her back.

By early September the Orioles found themselves mathematically eliminated. Then he started playing better—everybody did. The pressure lifted—everyone knew they were losers, at least that year, so they gave themselves permission to just play.

During the last week of the season Van stood out in center field. During the night game clouds of moths swooped around the banks of lights, circling and flaming around them and diving into the light field and then back again. Van thought back to that time in Rochester when a brown bat flopped onto the grass and died. Van called the umpire. One of the ball girls scooped the poor creature up with her glove and carried it away.

He didn't often *savor*, he realized. He usually ignored the fans, the weather, and the *situation*. As much as he could. He just wanted to get the key hits, to make plays, to win. Van remembered Bud telling him once, "Kid, this seems like every day to you now, but it can all disappear quickly. Like that." He snapped his fingers. "Enjoy it while it's yours."

More than anything, Van wanted a ring. Nothing unusual in this. The year before they called Van up, the team won the series. The regular players glorified that year. "Magical." "Destiny." As if everything worked all at once. "Something was in the air." Luck? The hand of God? They had not managed to return to the playoffs since. He wanted to be a winner. He wanted to be *part* of something.

That night he felt wistful. At twenty-five, his whole career splayed out in front of him. He was the starting center fielder. Strong and healthy and filled with energy. And yet, Van felt cursed—as if the world decided who the winners would be ahead of time, as if the universe rebuffed him for some slight or minor offense.

If he *could* drink he would. He would drink a lot. Instead, he stared up at the moths circling the bank of lights. When a batter hit a foul ball, a few moths peeled off toward it, eventually returning to the masses. The ball must reflect light, Van thought.

Then Sly Bothan hit a ball high and deep, well over his head. Van raced back, but it sailed over his head, over the wall for a homerun. Van felt his forearms whack the wall. He braced himself. These walls, Van thought.

Obstacles.

Slim looked at him and Van tipped his cap.

"You okay?"

"Yeah, I'm good."

It was dark behind the fence. Van would rather not think about what lurked behind it.

A few fans booed. Shermie had a tough night. There was no luck about *that*. Van hoped to make his own someday. He inspected his cleats and ignored the stands, ignored the sky.

Watch the ball, he thought. It's all right there. Seams and stitches—it's all right there.

The Time Van Sabotaged His Chances with the Most Beautiful Woman in Town

When I played, you could find ladies everywhere. Baseball was big and football had not yet taken over the sports world like it has now and a legion of regulars hung around, asking for autographs, flirting with us after a game. We flirted back. They followed us to the bars and restaurants we frequented. A few even knew where we lived and hovered around out on the street waiting for us to step outside. Real money had just come into the game and we were stars. Not rich ones, but still stars in America.

The one big star, Jake, had it the worst (or best depending on your point of view). Also, Jimmy and even Bud. A strange subculture if you think about it—these women who wanted to sleep with ballplayers, the hangers-on to jock straps. As if they collected *us*, not just our autographs.

Most of these groupies, however, showed no interest in me. I'm not a handsome man by any stretch. I clean up well, but I have a disagreeable honker and bad skin and my hair always managed to look mangy and rumpled.

But then after a game (which we won) a girl approached me, head tilted—drop dead gorgeous, killer body, sweet as could be. She goes, "I've had my eyes on you for a long, long time."

I'm signing her autograph and she's leaning into me.

"Is that right?" I said.

"Yes, it is. Would you like to have a drink with me tonight? See what happens."

At this moment I could've just said yes. It was easy pickings. But for some reason I became hung up on the drinking part, which seemed like a recipe for disaster—since I didn't drink and she did.

"I'll just be drinking Coke or lemonade, if that's okay."

"That's….fine," she said. "Whatever you want. I don't care."

"You can get trashed if you want. It's not a problem. I'm just saying, I'll drink juice or soda."

"I won't get trashed," she said. "What do you think I am? You think I *like* this?"

Not sure what she meant by that.

She snarled, pivoted away from me and found another player on the team instead. There were plenty of other choices.

I blew it. I always found a way to blow it.

24

By October Van was actually glad the season was over. He still loved the game—and it was just a game, even if it paid the bills. But his second season left much to be desired—second place finish, underachieved. In some respects, they played better than the year before—even though they didn't have the same results. Van didn't. Batting .257 was not what he hoped for, and his power numbers dipped.

Bud sat him for part of August and September ("everybody needs a recharge now and then").

By October Van wanted to be anywhere but Baltimore. He retained no interest in the *Sun* or bumping into fawning fans in the street or have middle-aged men recognize him at Vicci's or MaCabby's Seafood. The fallen star. The baleful disappointment. The has-been. The never-will-be.

So Van returned home for a few weeks—packed his bags and moved in. As if he was fifteen again.

His mother cooked for him every night. He talked some baseball initially with pop but then dropped it—settled with playing pool in the basement. They could play for hours. His father still wielded the upper hand, probably always would.

He felt glad to be there. It felt right.

Then he got in his car with a suitcase and a bottle of water and drove. He didn't have any place in mind; he just wanted to go. Clear his head. See something different, change it up. He drove west into the mountains and ate meatloaf and potatoes at a place in town before finding a hotel where he could crash.

He wanted to forget all of the pressure, the expectations. He wanted to forget everything.

In the morning, he drank the thin coffee and ate toast and a mealy orange. He drove west through the woods, into vast expanses of corn and soybeans as far as the eye could see. He stopped to get gas and called his mother so she wouldn't worry.

"I'm on a little adventure, I guess," he said. "I just felt like letting the air blow through my hair for a bit, see something different."

"That's good, son," she said. "Enjoy life while you can, experience it all."

"Do you think I'll ever have a family? I'm not sure I'm a family kind of guy."

"I'm sure you will. You'll meet the right person somehow. Don't *worry*. That's the blockade—the worrying."

It has always been. Himself versus himself.

"Thanks, ma. That helps. At least somebody has confidence in me."

"We all do," she said. "You'll be *fine*. Don't worry so much."

Van enjoyed the feel of the road: just him and himself—some tunes and all that space. He could get used to the expanse, the unscheduled terrain. The openness of whatever it is he wanted.

He drove west and slept by the side of the road. He could smell the Mississippi. In the morning, he bought a loaf of Wonder Bread and a jar of peanut butter and some apples. Plenty to last him for days. He could live this way.

Van drove into the plains, stretched his eyes. He felt lonely at first and then less lonely once he saw the birds circling high in the sky. He knew all that space was an illusion; one could get lost in it.

He wondered what his high school buddies were up to. He wondered what happened to his teammates. Corresponding wasn't Van's bag. Out of sight, out of mind. He had not really thought about them in years, or if he did it wasn't purposeful. But sometimes he did think of them. Sometimes he felt guilty, but then it dissipated.

The scent of grass and wildflowers: Van slept at a rest stop off the highway. He locked up his car and felt okay with it.

He drove into the desert. As soon as he witnessed the blankness, he knew it was where he wanted to be. There was *nothing* there, exactly what he wanted. He wanted his surroundings scoured. He wanted to obliterate everything. He didn't even know why. Van stayed out there for a long time. He slept next to his car on the dirt. He had a blanket and enough water to last a few days. The stars. The darkness above.

He avoided thinking about baseball or anything really. Van just let things drop at his feet.

When he ran out of water he drove to the nearest town and bought some.

And he returned and waited and listened and watched and felt the loneliness seep into him. Into the pit of his stomach. He did this for days.

Then finally he thought: that's enough. I can go back now.

So he did. He took out the one baseball in the trunk and kept it on the seat next to him. He watched it roll with the motion of the car as he drove. Four seams. Two seams. Four seams. Two seams.

The Time Van Fell Asleep in the Outfield

And still caught the fly ball. It had been a long night followed by an early makeup game at 12:30. I had to be there for BP at 10:00. Couldn't believe it, but Bud wanted us up and at 'em. Can't say I blame him in retrospect, but at the time I felt steamed. The night before I painted the town red trying to meet Mrs. Boyle, striking out left and right. I struck out the next day on the field even worse.

I should've gotten some coffee or something, but I didn't. I stood out there and suddenly a wave of exhaustion hit me. I mean a tidal wave of exhaustion like I've never experienced. The crowd seemed distant and quiet. The sun hung somewhere behind a gray haze. It was difficult to focus, to even see straight. Next thing I knew darkness descended and I dreamt of that redhead from the night before—the one with the freckles on the bridge of her nose and the ever-so-slight sunburn on her shoulders. But she wouldn't look at me. She wouldn't answer my questions, no matter how many drinks I sent her way.

"Hey, how come *you're* not drinking anything?" She cocked her head. Even annoyed, she looked cute. Perhaps even more than cute.

"I don't drink," I said. "It's something I don't do."

"And you expect *me* to?"

I simpered.

"That way I have some advantage," I said. "I need it."

121

She squirreled up her nose and turned away. I shrugged. That's what ruined my chances, I thought. One stupid comment.

Then crack and a baseball headed for me at one hundred miles per hour.

Luckily it soared and I saw it rising above me. Luckily, I also only needed to take three steps to my left and it landed right in my glove.

I tossed it back to Jake at second, yawning.

Luckily for me there weren't any runners on the bases or anything.

I don't think Bud or anybody noticed. I was fortunate that time.

23

Sometimes everything happened all at once. At least this is the way it seemed to Van.

He was back in Rochester, and he felt cheated. Would he be just another player to experience a September thrill, a cup of coffee in the bigs only to spend the rest of his career laboring in small towns? Akron, Brevard, Toledo, Syracuse, Scranton, Erie, Kinsport, Norfolk. Could Van be destined for some other life? Should he go back to school, learn a real trade, something he could bank on? In the bitter cold of April these thoughts raced through his mind. Umpires cancelled games as a result of sleet and snow. His hands seemed permanently numb and he had a cough he simply couldn't kick. Every time he hit a ball, his hands stung.

But on May 6 Abe Skillton broke his shoulder diving into second base. The team needed an outfielder.

Van got the call. Electricity ran through his entire body. If he had won the lottery for ten million dollars it would have provided less of a thrill.

Van felt bad for Abe at first. When Van first came up Abe was the one to take Van under his wings. He didn't want him hurt. But still, this was his chance and it was only temporary. He better make an impression, he thought.

And somehow, things clicked. He *saw* the ball. In the field he honed his concentration—the ball circling toward him; he slowed his mind. At the plate, the seams jumped out at him—the ball looked like a ripe cantaloupe. In May Van hit .385. At that point nobody could extract him. He was *helping* the team.

22

What the hell am I doing? Van thought. I'm 22 and getting older every year. I'm a *minor league* baseball player. I'm *nothing*. I have accomplished zilch. I am zilch.

Van knew his thought-process could be overly cataclysmic. He knew his teammates had faith in *their* futures, belief that their day would someday come. But faith and belief were a game for shmucks, Van thought. Luck rules. The universe decides who will succeed and who won't based on some unseen and unknown quantity. Who knew why the team called Kyle Milton up last year? Kyle even spent some time platooning in right. Kyle isn't any better than me, Van thought. At all. He felt definitely slower and not as adroit in the field, though he had more power and consistency as a hitter. But he was unsteady in the clutch. Maybe not the best team player.

Van knew that skill obviously contributed to success, but other factors played in—skill and execution just *seemed* the most important. How a guy advanced—that was the place where luck jabbed its fingers into what should be reserved for skill.

"You make your own luck," Coach K used to say. "Give it a chance."

But Coach K was an Evangelical, constantly attempting to, in Van's view, sway him religiously. Jesus. The hereafter. Salvation. The spirit beneath the surface.

"If you have a good attitude it will take you through life."

It seemed Pollyannaish to Van. If he smiled *then* he'd hit a homer? Preposterous. If anything, self-criticism created the opportunity for adjustment. You can't adjust for the better if you are positive and unthinking.

But Van knew he needed to relax. He needed to take it easy, to stop and smell the roses—every cliché of this type sort fit him.

It would all get easier if he had a chance; a single chance—all he asked for.

He played well that summer. Not so much a belief in his abilities—though he possessed that instinctively. Rather, Van wanted to prove them wrong. Bud Billings was an idiot if he didn't see how much Van Boyle could help the team. His loss, Van thought. A smile and a prayer will only get you so far.

In the field he rarely committed an error. He smoked line drives everywhere. His clutch hitting was the best on the team. Call it arrogance? Maybe.

Still, no calls. He felt the pressure; he knew he was only *twenty-two*. He did the snap-comparisons. By twenty-two Willie Mays was already a big star. By twenty-two Johnny Bench was winning the MVP. By twenty-two Joe DiMaggio was hitting .346. By twenty-two Bob Feller won twenty-seven games a year. Van Boyle, on the other hand, was a big nothing. Famous was a world away.

Van felt impatient, raring to go. He wanted to make his mark. His nightmare was dying forgotten and alone in a forlorn ditch somewhere. He wanted to *be* somebody.

He talked to the owner of the Red Wings, Mr. John Stallings. Stallings said join the club. Welcome to humanity. Everybody who's everybody has the same wish. "Bide your time, kid." He called his parents and his father said he knew Van was doing great. "Keep at 'em."

Finally September came and he got the call—with ten others. Expanded roster and all. But that was almost expected. If he didn't at least get a September call he felt he would've jumped off a bridge. Van minimized; he poo-pooed.

"Hey, man," Lyle Alcott said. "You're going to the *bigs*. Don't forget that."

Lyle was a catcher so maybe he was smarter than the rest (or more foolish, one or the other). He saw the big picture, despite the tools of ignorance he wore on the field.

It registered: I *am* going to the major leagues, Van thought.

The first time he walked into the stadium was perhaps the greatest moment of his life. The grass looked perfectly green, perfectly manicured. The sun shone just so. The sky seemed so blue it almost hurt to look up into it. Better than the most ecstatic sex. Better than a million dollars: the feeling of walking from the clubhouse down the hall and out of the dugout and seeing the empty field.

Then instead of grubby brown balls, pristine white ones. Instead of a few hundred fans, thirty thousand. Instead of some guy diddling around on the organ, a whole huge sound system. Big scoreboard; free food in the clubhouse. Boxes of arm bands and hats and jackets—as many as he wanted.

In Van's first at bat he faced a guy by the name of Chris Diller, a lefty for the Tigers. He possessed a herky-jerky roundhouse delivery and threw a big curve and changeup. It was 2-2 and Van slapped a sharp grounder between first and second. The second baseman dove, knocked the ball down, but Van legged out the hit. The crowd roared—or seemed to (so much louder, so many more voices). Van asked for the ball. The first baseman clapped him on the back. Van looked at the fans. He wanted *this*. Every day of his life he wanted only this.

21

Van knew something was wrong: he completely lacked an appetite. He turned twenty- one in October and had been imbibing heavily, he knew that. He refrained from telling anybody that he'd lost his appetite. It simply didn't seem normal. He felt constipated, bloated and a dull pain reverberated through the right side of his abdomen.

He was out on the town with a few teammates when Van nearly passed out. He stood up and suddenly felt woozy and weak. He completely lacked strength, had to sit back down immediately.

"Are you okay, kiddo?"

"Hey, someone get him a glass of water or something."

Admitted to the hospital the next day. Van watched the doctor observe him from the shadows. They took blood tests, put him on an IV. "You need fluids badly," he said, leaning over him. "We'll be back to talk."

The doctor returned and told him. "It's your liver. You tested negative for hepatitis—all the different manifestations. However, it's likely you had an allergic reaction to medicine."

"I'm not *on* any medicine.

"Do you drink?"

"Just turned twenty-one."

The doctor said it's rare, but that some people have a *reaction* to alcoholic beverages. On top of it, alcohol, of course, put pressure on the liver anyway—something everyone knew. In short, Van would have to stop drinking. He could never drink a beer or a glass of wine or champagne. The doctor said he'd run a few tests to confirm. When the doctor returned he nodded solemnly.

"It's not the worst thing in the world. It's not everything."

"It is what it is."

It was what it was.

During the off-season Van bedded down in Hagerstown for the winter. He was hoping the next spring he'd get the call. Double A. The last stepping stone. But this news came as a blow, a dampener. For days he had no energy, no enthusiasm. All he could do was recline in the bathtub, listen to the erratic radio.

He called his parents but didn't tell them the news. They liked to each take a phone and talk at once. Endearing but chaotic. His heart raced. He could not bear to admit a single weakness. He wanted to be the golden boy. He wanted to please them. This seemed an impossibility, often.

It took several weeks to feel better, but he did. He regained his strength. He regained his appetite. Though he told his buddies he couldn't go out to bars, he went to see a few movies and sat at a café and drank coffee and water and ate French fries.

The doctor told Van about a health specialist in Baltimore who came up with a plan of action for his recovery. Van couldn't face it. He knew he should give the guy a call, but it seemed ominous and overbearing. He didn't feel he needed *guidance*, just time.

"What do you do for a living?" the doctor asked.

"I play for the baseball team."

"You don't say," the doctor said. "Good for you."

"I hope to make it to the majors one day. A cup of coffee at least."

"I'm sure you will," the doctor said. "You're still young and strong. Can you hit a curve ball?"

Van told him all about it.

"Slider?"

Van nodded, shrugged. Sometimes.

That winter, when he felt better, Van went on a date. Her name was Kelly, a cousin of one of his teammates, a guy named Flan Wister. Of Irish heritage.

She was the first person Van told about his condition.

"It's nothing to fret about," she said. "Booze only causes trouble anyway. It's a curse to many."

"But I'll be missing out," he said.

"Don't *worry*," she said, kissing him on the cheek. She ruffled his hair. Caressed his shoulders.

Kelly was Van's first true love—always so sweet and beautiful and kind. She spoiled him, driving over to his apartment and helping him clean up, doing his dirty dishes—even though she rarely ate there. She looked after him even if he had trouble looking after himself.

But after three months Kelly met someone else.

Van sat there at the coffee shop frozen, almost in tears. Kelly glanced away from him, fiddled with her spoon. He could barely *look* at her.

"I'm so sorry, that's the way it goes sometimes." He loved the way she said "Sweetie"—as if he *was* a sweetie. She seemed so authentically genuine. "It's just, sometimes you're too down on yourself all the time. It's hard work, too hard." She always smelled great. Lavender and lemon and this sweet brown sugary scent. Like ginger snaps or snickerdoodles.

"I'll relax," he said. "I'll try harder. I know I've been a real drag. It's hard sometimes."

"I'm sorry, Van," she said. She squeezed his hand, then she walked out the door. He watched her lift and drop each heel.

20

Van barely scraped by and he loved every minute of it. He worked as a professional baseball player. He made his living chasing down fly balls, swinging at fastballs and sliding into second base. It wasn't a lot of money, but enough to feed and clothe himself. What wasn't to love? He would have played for free really, as long as he could eat. Odd to suddenly receive a bi-weekly check for something he considered fun. Receiving a paycheck for baseball felt like he pulled one over on the gods. Playing a child's game for money.

He considered his life to be exactly as he planned it. All those years of practicing, all that hard work—it was beginning to pay off. He didn't honestly care if they paid him nothing compared to the big leaguers. He was twenty years old. What could be expected? Compared to his classmates, he lived large.

When they called he said he *knew* he did the right thing. Jaime said she missed having him around, and Craig said nobody but nobody could spin a joke like he could (even if Van didn't think he possessed a funny bone in his body at all, ever—never did). But after several months they stopped calling, and he stopped calling them, also. He lived in a new world now and they lived in the land he departed. The gap widened.

His new life: the field, hotels, the bus, dinners at diners, playing darts and shooting pool to kill downtime in strange, small cities.

Teammates. Attempting to improve.

His teammates seemed like a decent group, but they lacked chemistry. Once he arrived in Frederick, he realized quickly that his teammates were his primary rivals—not the players on the other teams. His teammates too wanted exactly what he wanted. Except in their fantasy he was not present. They were fish in a pool and the bigs could only pull a few up on occasion. Those who stood out got called up. As a result, few players *fully* cheered for the others. They didn't seem to care about winning the game—they only cared about how they hit, their stats. A nest of contention.

This dynamic became obvious about a month into the season. The Keys took a rainy ride up 81 to Harrisburg. Miserable experience— halting and slow and the bus felt stuffy and muggy both and Van sat there sticky and slick with his own sweat.

Rain washed out the first game of the series. It pounded ceaseless, relentlessly thrashing down in waves.

The next day was sunny and clear and dry and the game started on time. Van watched the flags whip in center field, the air light and sere.

He felt nervous; he felt watched. Van hated that feeling. He could feel the eyeballs creep up his back, tingling. When Van entered the bathroom he needed to retreat to a stall, pee-shy. He loathed dressing or undressing in front of his teammates. When he took a shower, he kept his clothes at easy reach. Nobody would see him naked if he could help it.

After a while he would forget about the eyes on the field, get used to them. Early on in the game, he felt convinced his father sat in the stands, judging him, making notes from dark corners. An image of his father haunted Van: his chin perched between his hands, seemingly bored, his eyeballs darting in rapid-fire motion.

During this game in Harrisburg the image seemed to hang ever closer to his eyes. Van struck out three times and hit a weak pop-up. Van just felt thankful that the other team did not hit the ball to him at that time, other than a single lazy can of corn, which he easily gloved.

As a general rule of thumb, Van detested small-talk, but he also knew that in some situations he had to. This was one of those situations.

That night he had dinner with his roommate, Louie. Yet another greasy spoon. They both ordered meat loaf and potatoes.

"I just couldn't get it out of my mind," Van explained. "Couldn't concentrate on anything else. Which makes no sense because he'd never come up here to watch me. He never leaves."

"Things happen. I get distracted by the vendors sometimes," Louie admitted. "Popcooooorn, peaaaaaaaaaanuts. Right as I'm trying to swing. Isn't that ridiculous?"

"We have to block it out."

"*Have* to block it out."

But as Van stared at the ceiling that night he knew it was easier said than done. Everything was, really.

He counted to 1,000, then scrolled backwards, trying to fall asleep. His father grinned. He clamped his eyes shut, but all he could see: his father's incisors.

Van gripped the hotel comforter, pulled it to his chin, over his head. After some time he fell asleep, only to awaken again with the same image in the darkness, behind his eyes somewhere in darkness.

It was Dog Day at the park. Hot—ninety-eight and humid and the air sizzled and the fans lumbered like automatons through the shade, waving at themselves with their programs and newspapers and cardboard drink holders. It felt so hot it took everything Van had to make it through batting practice, the radiant heat from the empty aluminum bleachers making the heat even more unbearable.

Then during the game, the dogs howled in the stands. His team won 3-1, but even Van felt bored by the game. Three sacrifice flies scored the sum of their runs that evening. The bulk of the game consisted of pop-ups and strikeouts.

In the outfield Van wondered if he did the right thing. He quit college in January, after a single semester (after earning all A's and B's) and then he baked in the sun for a grand a month. He missed the closeness with his father. He wanted to pick up the phone and run his ideas by him, use him as a sounding board at bare minimum, vent. He wished his father did not suffer so much from rigidity, from being rooted in the past. *This* was his life now. Van wished his father could see that and find a way to nod his head and take it.

After the game he ate a couple of hamburgers with Jimmy, Sal and Ed. Sal was his roommate—their number two starting pitcher and an Italian from New York. His nickname around the locker room was Naples Sal as a result of the pride he carried for his Italian ancestral hometown. All nineteen and twenty—kids on their own, traveling around the country.

They drank a pitcher of beer. Then they drank another.

Back in the hotel room Sal and Van sprawled in their separate beds talking about what they missed most about home: baked ziti and fresh parm for Sal, and his little sister, Vicki—
his most ardent fan. She attended the majority of his games in high school.

"Well, you're lucky. I wish I had a sister," Van said. "Must be nice."

"Being an only child—is it lonely?"

"I don't know any different, so I can't really say. A lot of expectations from my parents. I can tell you that. A lot of weight. A lot of turmoil."

"I bet."

Van said he missed his mother. "She's a good one," Van said. "Best mother ever."

He felt woozy from the beer. His head felt heavy. Bloated.

Van thought back to the howling dogs.

"That was some funny shit wasn't it?"

"Minor leagues."

"Minor leagues."

"You glad to be here instead of college?"

"I think so," Van said. "One shot at this. Right?" He felt excited but also apprehensive—sometimes more of the latter.

"Right."

"Can always go back to school another time, right?"

"Sure. That's right."

18

Van spied them in the bleachers—the guys taking notes.

"Don't even look at them," his mother advised. "Black them out. They are only *dessert*. Something for after the main course."

That's exactly what they were, Van thought—dessert, the hopeful end result. Far away, down the road.

His father told him the opposite. At dinner one night Van's father banged his fist on the kitchen table, upending a cup of tea.

"You make an impression on those guys. They are *the* ticket, the only ticket. Nobody else can get you there." A vein throbbed blue on his temple.

132

Van nodded slowly. His mind stalled. He had no interest in talking about money or his future any longer; he knew that. The back of his neck felt sweaty and his scalp itched. He wanted to hit baseballs.

The batting cage: his constant refuge. His father used to pitch ball after ball to him—he couldn't forget about that. Despite everything. But in his senior year, Mr. Hank, one of the assistant coaches threw him extra and often BP, also. That helped a ton—all those reps. Working on his batting stroke.

Red stitches in the sunshine. That's all he saw.

Wood meeting stitched leather.

Line drive over the shortstop's head. The ball into the net. He could hit all day.

In school Van did well enough to make the honor roll, not well enough to be a standout or to earn an academic scholarship. He was slightly above average; he tried hard.

Mr. Scheller told Van that he should go to college. Class was over—world history. The blackboard appeared a scrawl of chalk— Alexander the Great's expansion.

"You're far too smart to just piss it away," Mr. Scheller said.

"I have baseball, also. That's my main plan."

"I know you can do both. And if you earn a college degree you'll have that in your pocket forever as well. You can always use it. And you'll still be young at twenty-one."

Van shrugged. He needed to get laid—that was a certainty. It had been too long. He felt this constant pressing need.

The most important thing of all was what was happening right now.

Sherry blew him off again. She said she could barely take Van's detachment any longer. Nothing was ever easy. Ever. Ever.

Tomorrow, he told himself. He would hit the ball for those men. He'd show them what he possessed burning inside. He'd show them who he was internally.

133

Sherry was not just another girl. Everyone knew Van as one of the glimmering stars, a high school stud. In the pantheon of seventeen year olds he hovered near the top. But Van could see that Sherry didn't take it too seriously—she seemed grounded, relatable. He liked this about her. He almost needed some element of *disrespect* in a girl he liked; he disdained moony eyes.

Van met Sherry in homeroom, which nobody, including the teacher, expected much from. But it functioned as a time for Van to do his homework or take care of last-minute readings. Most kids just socialized or took furtive naps. Mrs. Partridge seemed fine with naps as long as kids took them in the upright position. "Up, up, up," she'd say.

"What's the point?" Sherry said once. She said it to herself really but later she'd admit that she wanted Van to hear, also.

"What's that?"

Van shoveled his way through several math formulas—he procrastinated terribly with math in particular. He had eight more problems to finish before second period started and he found himself stuck and unglued already.

"It's not even busywork. It's just a time-filler."

Van shrugged, as if to indicate *I'm getting things done; I don't know about you.*

"You're Van Boyle, right?"

He nodded, trying to black her out. Sherry was "cute," but he didn't think of her as a *catch*, per se. She was just always around. Sherry being Sherry, one of those bony girls with bangs. On his list of beautiful girls at the school she didn't even make the top forty. He knew there was more to girls than looks, but at seventeen looks came first. Smart too— wry, incisive comments.

"Don't be rude," she said.

"What?" He lifted his head.

"Am I being rude?"

"You're not listening to me."

"I am, but I'm trying to finish these last few equations before the shit hits the fan. You know, important."

"It's *not* important though," she said. "One month from now you won't even remember anything about them. But you'll remember *me* for sure."

Van felt stunned by her bold statement, her sense of perspective. She thought big picture. She seemed to be attempting to imprint herself upon his cranium.

They went out that weekend, a movie then making out in the back seat. She made it into the top twenty based on personality alone.

And she was right. He *would not* remember those equations. And he would remember her. Unquestionably.

"You need to get out of that house," she told Van. "Your parents are suffocating you. It's clear. Whatever you do, make it somewhere else."

"That's the plan."

"They have you beaten down, like an old dog. You're far away…."

Van shrugged, nodded. "I guess."

He felt sincere.

They made love a month later. Van told her that he did, *probably*, love her. Whatever that meant.

"I probably do, also," she said.

Qualifications. Hedges.

They broke up in late June.

"I need more than 'probably' now, that's the thing. I need solid."

Van wanted to throw himself off a cliff he hurt so bad inside.

Instead, he went to the batting cage and didn't come out for three hours. His hands felt blistered and raw. Next day, same thing. Until he could barely lift his arms.

Was the time when my newspaper teacher, Mr. Robinson, was out on indefinite sick leave. Nobody knew for sure what the problem could have been. Some said his arm needed amputation. Others said he lay prostrate in a coma in the hospital. The rude jokesters said he was really a woman on maternity leave. Others said no, he caught mono from intimate relations with Carrie Knepper.

Me and my friend Kurt skipped class by explaining to the long term sub that we needed to squirrel away in the library, do research on some article we worked on together—the title changed each week. Spiders in the lockers. The dangers of fluorescent lighting. The legend of the hill monkey. The history of field parties. For some reason the sub never questioned them or their articles.

A thing of beauty.

It was simple: we would hop in Kurt's car and drive into the dark recesses of the county or head to the mall arcade or drive to town and steal miniature antique cars from Jerry and Son's vintage shop.

Only once were we caught—when the vice principal just happened to be out in the parking fetching something from the trunk of his car.

My mother waited, hand on hip, eyebrows narrowed. And that was that.

16

I won't always be alone, Van thought. He woke up at five-thirty every morning to hit the weights. Coach K said developing more upper body strength could be Van's clear rate to success, so that's what Van would dedicate himself to do. He joined the Y. He used the Y. He set goals. He met goals. He lifted for an hour, drove home, ate a quick breakfast, caught the cheese bus to school.

136

At night he swung the weighted bat two hundred times. He needed stronger shoulders, stronger wrists.

Van's father watched him sometimes. Out of the corner of his eye Van could see him lurking, watching him.

His father couldn't help him anymore, Van thought, but he could still make Van feel inconsequential—an insect pinned to a board.

The shadows inside looked angled and opaque. His father's starched dress shirts. The reflection off his platinum watch band.

He did well at school, well enough.

"I am proud of you every day," his mother said. "Every single day I'm alive. Don't forget this."

The last part sounded foreboding to Van, but he couldn't imagine anything ever happening to his mother. She was what Mr. Mercender called a "constant." She would live a long life and when he found himself rich and famous he would take care of her, buy her a fancy car, a condo on the beach.

When he returned home from school she always stood in the kitchen with a plate of sliced apples and sour cream potato chips and a cold can of soda. She would drive him wherever he needed to go. She would buy him whatever he desired—clothes, additional bats and gloves, anything. She would do anything for him.

Van's father barked at her if she was out too long. Van knew she must feel free, liberated from the confines of house and yard.

"Mom, do you think I can do it? I mean, really."

She knew what "it" was.

"Yes. Yes, I do. I *know* you can. You work so hard and you will be so great. I just know it deep down."

He leaned into her.

Van did not know exactly *why* he wanted to be famous. He had no idea where he found his drive. Did he desire further attention and love? Van wanted to ask his mother all about it, but he struggled understanding how to put it into words, even for himself.

She rarely mentioned her husband to Van, especially in his absence. But this one time she admitted to him that not everything is always as simple as it looks.

"Don't let your parents drag you down in life," she said. "That's a real danger—getting hung up on the past."

"In a few more years I will be on my own, I hope.

"But don't let us weigh on you. Me or your father, especially."

"I won't."

"You promise? I mean I would feel guilty if we sidetracked you. We could easily do that."

"I promise," Van said.

On the day he turned sixteen, Van took his driver's test.

He had enough allowance money saved up to buy himself an old junker.

That day he drove off into the countryside with the windows down. He yelped into the wind and drove as fast as he could. Corn and trees whizzed by. He was almost there.

15

"I don't want to talk to you," Van's father said. "Just do what you're supposed to do for once."

Van thought he had already become fairly good at that, without prodding. Why did his father feel the need to pile on? He already won.

"Okay," Van said. He knew better than to contradict—this got him nowhere.

"I'll be *watching*."

His favorite catch phrase.

Early March. The grass appeared brittle, tinged brown still from winter—only slight hints of green. Foreshadowing of spring.

Van ran suicides between second and first, a round of ten and then fifty pushups. Then back to suicides.

This was *his* idea, not his father's.

Van wondered if his father enjoyed making him nervous. He did. He knew he did. Thankfully, he rarely came to watch Van play. That would be a *real* intrusion. Van wondered if his father was possibly more a symbol at this point than a real person to him.

"And you're not getting squat afterward," his father said.

Van didn't need squat. Especially from him. He didn't need the additional layer of pressure, most of all.

He just wanted to sink into that trance-like state, watching the ball out of the pitcher's hand, the ball striking the bat. He didn't want to slack into laziness. All this—the weights, the training—was to him a way to push away indolence, at bare minimum.

His father held a ten dollar bill in two fingers and stood up so Van could see him. Van dug as fast as he could through the infield.

"For later, if you try," he said. "If not, I spend it on myself."

When Van was done with his workout his father ripped up the ten spot directly into Van's face.

"Nope, you don't get it now."

"Neither do *you* now," Van said. His father smiled, teeth shiny.

"I have many more where this came from. How about you? You can't even drive yet. Moron."

His father jabbed Van in the gut and walked off.

Van roiled in pain, curled down. It felt as if his stomach consumed itself. He reclined on the cold grass for a long time. He could hear distant birds. He couldn't think about anything but the pain.

When he felt he could manage it, he lifted himself. He could see his father's car idling in the parking lot. Its headlights glared.

Van walked one foot in front of the other. He told himself this was it, the end of the line as far as his father was concerned. He couldn't take it any longer.

Opening the door, Van sat down. His father said nothing to him. Just drove. Van turned a heat vent onto his face. He didn't know he would get punched for that, too.

14

In Van's reoccurring nightmare he stood at the top of a mountain when the ground slipped. He felt his feet loosen, as if he wobbled on a conveyor belt. Trees and rocks and animals slipped forward and forward until they all, at once, tumbled over the edge of the precipice and fell for a long time into the void. In the dream Van thought he would awaken when he began falling, but he didn't. Every terrifying moment of the fall could be observed right there happening to him.

And when he landed, it would not be onto rocks or water but instead into a pool of thick, grainy mud. He had to slog out of that, grunting, pulling himself to harder ground. But he was alone in the darkness, stalactites and stalagmites. Bats twittering in the nooks.

He shouted but nobody answered. Not even an echo. He was utterly alone.

This is when Van awoke.

Van possessed no inclination to mull over himself, but he found himself somehow doing just that. He didn't want to be yet another self-absorbed jerk. Maybe he was one anyway, or would be. He had no interest in pondering the future filled with question marks. Question marks hovering over the question marks. Maybe if he had a sister or brother, but as the only child he couldn't see an easy way out. He avoided mirrors, unless he had to apply gel to his frizzy hair—something to tamp it down. In this case Van nitpicked, smoothing down his curls in an attempt to fit in—though Van did not want to think of it in that way.

Van maintained dreary premonitions all the time. Where did these come from? Was his father poisoning his brain? He felt polluted, mentally ruined, his premonitions negative and sullen, pointing to a kind of desperation. Van wanted so badly to be taken into the fold, but he seemed confined to the fringes. Always, continually.

One of his premonitions had to do with tumbling down a long ramp. Two weeks later he fell down the stairs. His father snickered in his office at the top of the stairs. Van could hear him push away from his desk—then a full belly laugh. Van held his stomach and head at the bottom of the stairs, embarrassed and in pain.

Another premonition: somebody would stab him in the back—emotionally. Two weeks later his best friend, Mick, for some reason, started a rumor that Van stole two thousand dollars from his parents. In the account that trickled its slow way to Van, Mick's parents took him to court. Not a grain of truth to the rumors.

They hadn't spoken since.

Devastation. If Van's girlfriend (if he even had one—which he did not) dumped him, it would have had a lesser impact, by a long stretch.

Van's neighbor, Mr. Williams, invited Van over for iced tea on occasion.

"You need to learn how to *survive*," Mr. Williams said. Retired gym teacher.

"I do?"

"Just in case anything happens and you find yourself, you know, stranded. It's important."

Mr. Williams lent him survival books and shuttled him out into the patchy, poison-ivy strewn woods for mini-lessons.

After several weeks Van turned to Mr. Williams and proclaimed: "I can see how this is important. I just don't really have time."

"I'm sorry to hear that," Mr. Williams said. "I hope you never need it. At least I taught you a few small things."

Mick called Van later, but Van refused to budge.

"I'm apologizing, Van," he said. "Don't be so stubborn. This is me with an honest effort, trying to make it better."

"This will be the last time we talk." And it was. He hung up the phone. Survival. Yes, survival.

It was a dare, really. My friend Carl said there's no way I'd ever do it. But I was thirteen and I didn't care as much as I once did or would later. As class ended, I approached Mrs. White, sixty something, perennially grouchy, a year or two from retirement. Then I planted a kiss on her cheek and pulled back. I barely expected this either.

I hoped I wouldn't find myself suspended, expelled, and cloistered away in some back warren of the school.

She hushed and waved me off. She smiled at me, embarrassed perhaps, but mostly it appeared she wanted to brush it under the rug as a mistake. "You cannot be doing that, Van," she said. Over and over. I knew he might be fine then. And I felt twenty bucks richer—and a hero for an hour, at least. Until they all moved onto the next exciting thing.

13

Yes, they fought, but they were also best friends. That's what best friends sometimes did, Van knew.

They stood around in the backyard tossing around the football. Van was clearly the superior receiver, but Mick possessed the better arm by far. Van ran patterns and Mick zipped the ball to him in crisp arcs.

Mick asked Van how he could make the inter-county squad—an all-star baseball team. It was a big deal to make it—a difficult achievement. The team included Van at the early age of twelve. "A sure sign of stardom," his mother said. His father chomped on his grilled cheese sandwich.

"Just help me out," Mick pleaded.

Van told him it was relatively simple: he needed to perform well at tryouts. That's it. That's the entirety of it. Mick wanted to know every *aspect* of the tryouts in advance, but Van admitted he couldn't tell him for certain because coach changed it year to year. But he did tell him what he did the year before.

When it came time for tryouts, Van smacked line drives all over the field. He *cracked* the ball. He never felt faster on the base paths or on the timed sprints. In the field, everything which soared his way, he caught.

"I performed just okay," Mick said. His own evaluation. He feared jinxing his possible success, he said. But he needed to be honest with himself, with Van.

When Coach posted the names, Van's name appeared on it. Mick's did not.

Kids staring at a list of names. All the power there.

Van tried to call him, to console—they talked every night, phone cords stretched down the hall, around bed posts. Talking girls and baseball and school—if they ran out of things to say about the first two. Mick didn't feel like talking that night.

"What's with you two?" Van's father said once. "Only *girls* talk on the phone. What do you have that is so interesting to talk about?"

"I don't know," Van said. He didn't think he needed to justify; he wanted to change the subject.

"What?"

"We fight a lot, I guess," Van admitted.

"Arguing or punching?"

"Both, but more arguing. The phone makes it better."

"Oh, Jesus Christ," his father said. He clenched and unclenched his fist, a nervous habit.

Van remembered the day his father chased him around the house with a stick he found in the yard. He said he wanted to try it out. The stick looked longer than a baseball bat and thicker with knobs and pointy ends and abrading bark.

"Looks like a great whacking stick," he said.

His father displayed a sarcastic smile on his face. He said he would "dispense some wisdom." That's what he did, freely.

Mick dropped by a few days later and tossed the football around again. This time Van was quarterback and Mick was the receiver. They

143

hung out at Mick's house. They drank Pepsi and ate Cheetos after. They played ping pong. Everything seemed fine. All the time, fine.

12

At Mick's birthday party Todd sat to the right of Mick. Van sat across the table with the tier two friends nibbling on half-stale potato chips. Mick's mother sat rigid to Mick's left, lavishing him. He joked that he was still a Momma's boy. His father was not really in the picture—though he popped in and out of his life from time to time. Mick avoided elaborating much on his feelings or opinions. The closest he came: the time he admitted his father still sent him gifts and called. "That's about it," Mick said.

"You can have mine," Van said. "I don't need them."

At the birthday party the kids ate pizza and hot dogs and his mom brought homemade pickles and coleslaw and fried tomatoes.

They played darts in the basement and billiards, though Mick seemed to be the only kid who knew how to play. Van could barely sink a ball. The other kids complained that nobody likes a lucky, spoiled kid with his own pool table. Nobody. Mick stuck both middle fingers up and the others mirrored him.

Van's gift to Mick was a new baseball glove, but when Mick opened it he said, "Nope, wrong kind." He had no need for another Rawlings, he said; "they're too stiff—too wooden for me."

"Sorry," Van said. He constantly felt filled with remorse and inadequacy and envy.

The other kids, whose parents made more money or who gave them a larger allowance, gifted Mick video game systems or remote control helicopters or bats or stacks of records. Unbelievable.

Johnny gave Mick an air hockey table and Mick acted so excited he gave Johnny a high five three times and almost hugged him—that didn't escape Van's notice.

144

Van wanted to tell Mick how much he meant to him, how he was the only friend who mattered. He imagined all the other boys fell into a pool of lava—that it was just Mick and Van left. They could use all the games and equipment and have a great day without the rest.

But when he lifted his head they were all still there, his glove in the corner. Van put it on. The others turned toward Mick. They blasted rock and roll and drummed their jeans and pounded their pool sticks on the basement floor over and over. A rhythmic incantation, some cloaked bestial ritual.

11

When things didn't go his way, Van skulked out back to whack sticks against tree trunks. He did that a lot. He liked to think it helped his swig, his hand/eye coordination. He had no idea if it did. Van just knew he liked the *feeling* of the stick breaking in his hands. That alone gave him a boost. Then, if still enough sticks lay around, he'd thwack more. The bark bore the marks.

"What's with all the racket?" His father shouted from the deck.

Van shrugged. He knew better than to get into a debate with his father. Lose-lose with hell to pay later.

"What do you think they grow on trees?"

His father laughed at his own joke. Van didn't. Van smacked another branch against a tree trunk. His mother was attending a PTA meeting.

When he bounded inside for dinner, his father shoved him into a corner with one stiff arm.

"I have something to tell you. Are you ready?"

"I'm ready," Van said. He clenched his fists in anticipation.

"You're a hot shot now, so let me break it to you. You're my son, but seriously. You're such a little pussy. You know I have no idea if you're really mine. You could be. Then again, maybe not. See what I'm saying? I

145

doubt my son would be such a weakling. It's not in my genes." He grabbed at his own groin.

Van pushed away from him and bolted up the stairs, but his father followed him. Van could smell his hunger, his competition.

Van locked himself in his room, but his father had the key.

"Ah-hah, surprise!"

"I don't want to *talk* to you," Van said. "You're messing with me."

"Let me tell you something," he said.

Here we go again, Van thought. The stream of bullshit wisdom never ceased.

"You think it's all about you. It's not. There are two adults who live here. Both of us have our stories, our own problems."

"I know that," Van said.

"So just shape up and try not to be a wastrel," his father said. His father liked to use that word, Van knew. Wastrel. "We have seven more years and then you're out on your ass."

His father told him that even though he may or may not be his biological son he would treat him as a son no matter, with love. That's the thing to do, he said. "And sometimes you have to do the thing to do. I don't love you."

Van thought of the trees in the wind.

"Can I go to sleep now?"

"No, we're going to play a game," his father said. "Think of this house as a track. You're going to run around it in circles and I'm going to chase you. Are you ready?"

"Jesus," Van said. "Not again."

"Don't take the Lord's name in vain."

"You're not religious."

"On your mark. Get set. Go!"

And Van ran, even though he didn't want to. He ran through the open door as fast as he could and down the hall and into the living room

146

and his father chased him, lumbering, thumping, and Van circled back through the kitchen, evading him, and back upstairs.

But he knew. Van knew eventually his father would catch him. He knew it was only a matter of time—unless he ran out the front door and down the street, which he had done before. But save that, his night seemed over.

The Time Van Wasted a Day

I usually tried to be painfully efficient, to a fault. I admit it. I took care to finish homework on time, to be dutiful, to complete my chores when asked. I tried to be good and thought of myself as such. I wanted to be thought of as responsible and honest, even if I occasionally slipped. These occasions were rare.

It was a cool day in October. I woke up and felt relaxed and low-energy and unable to fully concentrate on anything resembling real work.

I walked to the park half a mile from my house and found a willow and sat in the shade and then reclined in the grass and stared up at the sky through the canopy and watched the pointy leaves fall around me and land on me. I didn't care. I followed a contrail across the patch of sky and fell asleep. I dreamed about girls and the red seams of a baseball rotating to me, endlessly. My bat meeting the ball sharply. The crack of wood. My first step toward a sprint.

10

"You want to be a ballplayer, is that right?" Van's Uncle Al liked to press him. Uncle Al seemed interested in his future, curious about his doings. Even though Uncle Al only saw Van once a year at the family reunion, he pressed for the latest details.

"How do you know?"

"Your mother, of course! We talk, also."

The family sat by the glittering, gleaming water. The wind blew steady, but not hard. Most of the older relatives wore caps or sunhats and

147

sunglasses. They ate cantaloupe and grilled chicken and pasta salad and corn.

"I don't want to go," Van had said back at the house. But he relented; he felt embarrassed.

"You know everyone wants to *see* you," his mother remarked. "They like watching you grow up. We all do."

He didn't want to "be seen" though. She argued that if he planned on existing in the public eye as a famous baseball player (no sarcasm in her voice) he needed to get used to what the people want. He had to occasionally cater to whims. He had trouble following the argument entirely. Plus, his father never attended. Why should he? Sacrifice a whole day?

But Uncle Al acted sweet and doting (he slipped him a ten dollar bill, calling it an "investment"). And Aunt Lilly's baked beans shone as the star of the show and she never pinched his cheeks and she looked him in the eyes and listened to him carry on about school and the woods and baseball. Aunt Clarice drank too much white wine and hugged him one too many times, but he suffered through. Eventually her eyes became glassy and slipped away.

Maybe the reason why he couldn't muster more excitement to attend a family reunion: his maternal grandparents showed little interest in him. His grandmother chain smoked and ignored his questions and played cards with her relatives. "How're you doing, kid?" he wondered if she knew his name. As for his grandfather, he slung horseshoes and drank Busch and never even came over to greet Van. Just a quick wave from afar and then back to laughing with the adults.

Luckily one of his cousins brought Wiffle ball, so playing that was an option. The ball floated and dipped and knuckled, but Van squared up on it every time and drilled it long and deep. The ball whistled in the gnatty air and he ran as fast as he could through it.

His mother kissed his forehead in the car.

"Thank you for coming. It meant a lot to me."

Van slept on the ride home and woke up woozy and disoriented.

His father sat in the La-Z-Boy, the television glow the only light. His back thick and broad. Van crept up to bed, while his mother caressed her husband's arm as if smoothing a carpet. As if brushing dust from a piece of furniture.

9

I am *happy*, Van thought; I have Mick, my best friend and Sarah, who kissed me and Christie who also likes me, in case it doesn't work with Sarah, and my mom loves me and I can play baseball and be happy.

Van's father held off for a while. That helped.

"He doesn't mean anything by it. You know he loves you. He always has, always will," Van's mother said.

"Okay," Van said. He found it easier to give short answers. The less he said the better off he would generally be. It's difficult to get in trouble for being an unobtrusive pipsqueak.

They sat at the kitchen table. His father sat in the other room, watching television. He watched a lot of television those days. Van wondered if his father felt happy in his marriage. He wondered if his parents would someday get divorced like some of the parents of his friends. He had no idea how he would react to that.

His mother poured him a second glass of chocolate milk, holding her finger to her lips.

Keep it between us.

"I've been meaning to talk to you for a while now, about some of the things that he does. I know he's not easy on you."

"Why don't I have a brother or sister?" Van asked. "That would make things different." A pertinent question—he never knew the answer, but he wished he had one. If he had a sibling he would have somebody to help him along, someone to confide in. Maybe his father wouldn't feel quite so free to haul off.

"I don't know," his mother said, sitting across from him. "We did try, but it hasn't happened yet. But you never know. Would that make you happy?"

"Yes," Van said.

"Does it get lonely being alone, the only kid in the house?"

"Sometimes," he said. True.

"What I wanted to say is that he's not always fully in control, if you know what I mean. He is guided sometimes. It's hard to explain."

Van drank his chocolate milk. This was one of the times not to talk more than he needed to, Van thought. He listened to the sly buzzing of the refrigerator.

"I try to bring him back to the good side, but I'm not always the most convincing," his mom said. "He has a way with words. He can really sling them together, can't he?"

Van shrugged.

"Well, you're not saying much. Are you okay? Is this too hard to talk about?"

Van shrugged.

"I'm sorry if this isn't the life you want. Someday you'll be older and you'll have a way to understand all of this. And then you can do things your way. It's difficult being a kid sometimes. You can feel trapped in the life around you. I remember that feeling."

Van couldn't think of himself as anything but nine—maybe ten—since his birthday wasn't too far off.

He softly pushed the empty glass back to his mother and stood up.

"Where are you going?"

"My room. I'm tired."

His mother stared at him for a long time.

"What?"

"Nothing," she said. "That's fine."

And in his room he played the radio softly and pressed his ear to it. The beat thumped steadily. It rocked him and he drifted off.

The Time Van Ate Ants

I went through a phase where I didn't like the taste of meat, just didn't want to eat it. It was fine; my mother seemed happy to oblige—she liked beans and vegetables and she could cook those for me any time I wanted.

I detested the thought of eating animals; I liked them too much— I guess I had a soft spot.

But I felt frequently weak and sometimes faint and my mother admitted that despite my best intentions I might need more protein somehow.

"Tofu and eggs will help; I'm not sure they will be enough though."

I remember one game. Hot and humid and dusty and I possessed zero energy. I saw an anthill in the outfield and I slipped my finger into it. The ants raced up my arm and I licked them off it, as many as I could. I could feel them on my tongue. Quick swallows helped. Luckily, nobody hit the ball to me in that inning, very lucky. Ants scurried all over my arm and torso and still did when I ran into the dugout to bat. I didn't try that again for a long time.

I was a kid.

8

Van had a crush on the new girl. Her name was Sarah Hollen, the cutest girl in the class. He wasn't sure of her nationality, but she had brown skin and dark hair and her pupils looked a murky coffee brown. There weren't many girls like her in school, Van knew. She was nice, also—she smiled at Van a lot and she didn't mind if Van sat next to her.

Mick liked Sarah, also, but since he was best friends with Van he let him have the first shot at her. Their top twenty list was fluid and pretty soon Sarah sat at number one on Van's, but Mick said he didn't think she looked *that* cute. Cute, but not as pretty as Debbie or Julia or Wendy, in particular.

Van brought her two quarters one morning, as a kind of sweet, romantic gesture.

He thought flowers would be too obvious, and who doesn't like quarters?

"Thank you," she said and put the quarters in her pocket. But that night Sarah's mother called Van's mother on the phone. She told Van all about it. She complained about the gift and said that her daughter can't accept it. Her love is not for sale; she is not a whore.

"I'm insulted, frankly," she said.

Van's mother smiled wryly and shook her head, reporting this.

"I know you didn't mean anything by this," she said. "But she's giving you the fifty cents back. Next time, try flowers or something."

A week later Van built up the courage in Mr. Frinthood's class to slide his fingers into Sarah's. She gasped but then clenched his fingers and squeezed them. Her eyes flitted. After a minute she withdrew her hand, but what a minute.

Mick and Van played Wiffle ball in the backyard. He felt bad that day because he knocked a line drive which glanced off Mick's head. Mick cried for a bit but shook it off and they continued. Sometimes they played down in the old drainage ditch; the earthen walls functioned as a natural fence. But that day they played in the backyard, where the shrub grew at shortstop and where the ball could thwack the siding of the neighbor's house—the neighbors seemed nice enough to not protest.

Van loved the whistle of the Wiffle ball and they played into the evening until it became too dark to see and even then they turned on the outdoor light and kept going until Mick's mom picked him up.

Van ate lasagna with his parents and a salad with tomatoes and cucumbers and warm peach pie for dessert. There was time for these things. Van was glad for it.

He just met Mick a few months before, since Mick's family just moved to the area. His parents had always lived in their house, and as far as Van was concerned they always would.

The Time Van Chased a Rabbit

I had to have pets. I needed to care for animals; I realized this early on.

We owned two cats and they lounged on my bed as I scribbled away at my homework. We had a dog though my father said she would be *my* problem since I was the one so gung-ho. I walked her every night—my mom helped out in the mornings. We had a parakeet. We had two gerbils, though they didn't live long. We had a guinea pig and a tank of goldfish. We had a lizard for a brief time, until it died.

When I said I wanted rabbits my mother bought me two and we kept the hutch in the backyard by the shed. I loved holding them in my lap, one at a time as I fed them lettuce and mustard greens and tomatoes. Their warm body weight against me.

One night I must've forgotten to secure the latch on the hutch; when I got up to feed them in the morning the rabbit I called Rooster could not be found.

Then I spotted him under the dogwood and ran to chase it. I ran as fast as I could to the boxwood, the elderberry, the maple—chasing Rooster. Then Rooster doubled back and ran behind the shed and under the hutch and then, finally, out onto the side of the hill where Rooster stopped to eat a dandelion. This is where I grabbed him.

Rooster and the other rabbit, Caveman, died a year and a half later when a tree fell on their hutch.

I felt cursed and, as a result, I no longer wanted rabbits any longer. I felt as if my bad luck would slay them.

They were on vacation in the mountains. Van was too young to know where. He just knew the drive was at least three or four hours from home—he slept a lot on the way there. They rented a cabin in the woods adorned with antlers and a stuffed bear in the corner, claws protruding. Van's cousins Jimmy and Kelly came along also, and his aunt and uncle from his father's side.

The first few days consisted of a blur of canoeing and hiking and campfires and long games of cards and board games at night. Van's parents let him carry a hatchet to collect kindling; he felt powerful. Lucky seven.

Their cabin overlooked a lake, and on the third night they all went swimming. Everyone went—even Van's dad who disdained it.

It was a stunning body of water—dark and shrouded by pine and spruce trees and speckled with lights from the cabins surrounding it. The moths flew over it and the bats followed and swooped down to them—a constant swooping overhead. At first, Van sprung off the pier and swam out to the little flotation dock fifteen feet away—the lake wasn't deep and his parents watched him. Van's cousins did the same and they began batting a beach ball around and laughing and playing makeshift volleyball without the net.

After a while the cousins and Van's aunt and uncle and Van's mom became tired or cold or both and decided to dry off and walk back up to the cabin and eat pie and drink beer and take hot showers to warm up.

"Wimps!" Van's father shouted.

"Yeah, wimps!" Van echoed.

In the water by the dock Van's father asked Van if he wanted to know the key to being a man.

"Yes," Van said.

"Give me your hand," he said. Van stuck it out.

His father lifted his head and waited and smelled the air.

After a bit Van's father guided his hand down to his stomach, then to his penis and slowly, methodically moved Van's hand up and down with his.

"You have to make it bigger to see what a man can really look like. You might look like this yourself someday, if you are lucky."

Van tried to pull his hand off but his father clasped his arm to his side and kept it there.

"I feel cold now," Van said.

"That ship has sailed."

Van didn't know what that meant. His father made Van do what he said. They were under water and nobody could see, Van's father said. They didn't know, but you can tell. You can feel what's it's like to be a man. Van did as he was told.

"We do this for each other sometimes. It's okay. Relieve the pressure. It's okay."

Van wanted to be a good boy; he did as his parents told.

After a while his father grunted and threw his head back and he pushed Van's hand away.

"Thatta boy," he said.

Van shivered in the water.

Van's father carried Van from the shore to the cabin.

"I don't want you to hurt your feet. There are things that can hurt you here," he said.

Van clung to his father's neck. It was thick and smelled of the fetid lake. The lights from the cabin danced through the trees.

Van didn't want to think about anything. He just wanted to slip into the blackness.

6

Flashlight tag on a summer night. Skipping rocks across the creek. The sweet scent of fresh cut grass. The dusty whirl of his bedroom window fan. Van's eyes bugged at the sight of the ocean spray, mountains cresting the tree line. Kickball, four-square, dodge ball.

He discovered t-ball by accident. Van looked for another dodge ball game—far too many kids jammed the first one. He walked up the hill to the clover field and Mr. Phillips stood up there, showing kids how to hit off a tee, impromptu. Not part of a class or an organized anything, just for fun.

At first Van just watched from the shadows, but eventually it became clear to him that a line existed and that he was in it.

The thwack of bat against ball—the ball sailing out into the humid air. The ball skidding on the grass until it rested in it. The ball rising and diving in the wind.

"You want to give it a try, Van?"

Van nodded.

Electric. He hit the ball and it flew out from him. He barely felt a thing—just the whoosh of the bat to and through the ball and back around. A tingling feeling. Goosebumps.

"Wow! Great job, Van. You're a natural!"

He told his mother about it and she listened, hands clasped on her lap. Her eyes looked heavy, as if she felt tired or had been crying the night before.

"I'm so glad you found something you love."

His father came home late, ate quickly, then disappeared into the basement. He owned a toy train collection and he was working on the town and the pasture just beyond it. Van wasn't allowed down there, but a few times his father brought him down and showed him his projects. But it sounded cacophonous and smelled of glue and Van felt peculiar there, as if the ground wasn't quite stable.

His father took Van to the YMCA the next morning. He swam there three or four times a week, diving under and then doing laps for forty minutes before work.

"You can swim in the baby pool while I'm doing laps," he said.

"I'm not a baby."

"We all know that, but you can't do laps with the adults."

So Van did as told, using his powers of imagination to keep himself interested. He imagined he sat on a sinking ship. He imagined he reclined in an underwater cave and needed to be rescued by his father. He imagined he lived as a sea serpent, slithering underwater.

But he felt lonely in the baby pool by himself, as lonely as he's ever felt. And when Van became cold and bored he stepped out of the pool and dangled his feet in the water, turning his head behind him.

His father climbed the ladder out of the lap pool and walked over to another man. The man pointed in Van's direction and his father smiled and his father laughed. They talked for some time. They stood close to one another as they talked, as if they whispered. They laughed and the man touched his father's arm and his father patted the man on the shoulder and looked around. Then Van's father walked over to Van.

"C'mon, let's go," Van's father said. "Let's get you out of that soaking wet bathing suit."

Van followed his father to the locker room. He didn't think anything of it.

The Time Van Stared at a Wall for Twelve Hours

I told my father he was a stupid head. That was the one thing my father couldn't abide, I knew that.

"Never, ever call me *stupid*," he said. "Go sit there and stare at the wall. Then we'll see who the stupid one is. It's you. You're stupid."

So I went and stared at the wall in the basement and I didn't fall asleep and I didn't bring a book or blocks or army men and I kept myself occupied by counting the indentations in the wall and counting the indentations on each section of the wall and then connecting the indentations in my mind; forming shapes and figures and then racing my eyes up and down the wall in patterns.

I found a way.

At ten at night my father opened the door to the basement (my mother visited her sister for the weekend).

"Dinner," he said. That meant his staring-at-the-wall session came to a completion. Kaput.

Dinner? Fish sticks and an unpeeled carrot. I peed and then sat at the kitchen table. My father watched television and I ate alone.

5

Van's father said he didn't like a baby. Van didn't cry. His mother said she loved it when Van helped out in the kitchen; he wanted to be a good helper.

Van was only just starting, they said. With school, with learning, with everything. No need to rush. Enjoy it. *Being a kid is fun!*

He watched them eat.

He watched them drink.

He watched them dance.

His parents were young and his mother looked so beautiful and he could entertain himself all day. He could just be.

The trees in the backyard seemed very old and looming and they cast heavy shadows over the house in the afternoon. His mother grew tomatoes and beans and squash and sunflowers. He helped her with these, also—especially the tomatoes. They tethered the plants to stakes and lashed the stakes to the fence.

Vines grew up one side of the house and he helped his mother pull them down off it.

"If you don't, they will make the house crumble," she explained. "That wouldn't be good if the house crumbled, would it?"

"No," Van said and pulled as hard as he could on a vine.

"Mommy, are these poisonous?"

"No," she explained. "You could probably even eat them, if you needed to. Some animals do at least. But don't try. Not now."

Van had a funny feeling in his stomach when she said this. She told him he did so great. She told him he was her favorite little boy.

And when his father came home they'd laugh in the kitchen and he would drink wine.

Only later would his father disappear.

When Van asked where to she pointed downstairs. She said he liked to be alone down there, like a troll under a bridge.

"Is he an ogre?" she asked Van.

"I don't know," Van said. "What is that?"

"They eat children for lunch," she said.

She gave him cake and milk and he sat at the kitchen table eating the cake and drinking the milk, where they smiled and laughed earlier. He listened to the sound of crickets and he felt sleepy and content. Life *was* sleep and contentment. He was an animal, a human animal.

4

Van could walk, he could talk. He could kick a ball and chase it. His grandparents liked to watch him—but they sat on the couch on the other side of the room. It was a large, spacious room, filled with light.

His favorite toy: a tractor, metal and green with a yellow seat. Thick grooved tires that would leave an imprint in the carpet when he ran the tractor in circles.

His grandmother gave him a roll of pennies to play with and look through. Van's mother glared at her; he wasn't sure why.

"Don't put those in your mouth," she said.

He liked the weight of the pennies in his hands, the different years, the different patterns on back—wheat and a large building and some of the years were old and made him think and a few pennies appeared pewter in color and his grandmother explained why.

They ate corn on the cob and hamburgers and slaw.

His cousins were all older than him and watched him, and played with him, but none of the cousins were his age so they became quickly bored and wanted to do more exciting things than hang out with a little kid. They started looking away, searching the room or the yard for something more interesting.

He tried to follow them outside but the gravel felt jagged on his tender feet bottoms. He hopped back inside, gingerly.

Van watched the hummingbird out the window. It darted in and out of the feeder, dipping down into the sugar water. He listened to the cicadas and felt the wind through the open windows.

He consisted of senses, no ideas. He was colors and scents, not feelings or thoughts.

His mother handed him a honeysuckle flower in the driveway, and he sucked the sweet sap from it. It was sweet and delicious, and Van wanted more.

3

Van received constant applause. For running. For throwing. For putting on his shirt. For taking off his shoes. For finishing his spinach. For finishing his cup of chocolate milk. He wasn't a baby. They said they felt proud of him and they clapped and told him how good he was, a big boy. A real big boy now.

He liked to hide under the bed, in the closet—make his parents find him. And when he hid in there he'd curl up into a tiny ball and laugh to himself. Almost overwhelming how funny it was. He put both hands over his mouth so that he didn't ruin the surprise.

But they found him—they always did, and he laughed so hard he sometimes lost all control.

His father liked to hide from Van. But Van always found him easily and his father seemed angry, or frustrated, but maybe he just pretended. Hard to tell how adults felt and exactly *what* they felt. Feelings seemed tricky, abstractions, something dangerous. He frowned a lot and his voice became loud suddenly.

Van's father liked to watch him from across the room, as he played blocks or cars or sat on the floor flipping through a picture book. Van hoped he would come down, join him. He only did if it was about winning. Then he crawled on the floor, on all fours.

At night his mother carried him up to bed, kissed his head, rubbed his back. Sometimes he couldn't sleep and she stayed with him.

The blankets felt heavy on him and sometimes he also felt hot. He never saw his father at night. Those were the times he vanished.

2

They competed, even then. This is one of Van's first real memories: his father tapping the red ball back and forth across the carpet. To get a point Van had to hit the ball into his father's knees, but he could use his hands to protect them. He played goalie. He hit his knees frequently, but then he could barely walk—Van had an excuse. Van competed before he could string together a cogent sentence.

Van's father would beat him every time, laughing at the results. It wasn't malicious or cruel laughter, but at age two it seemed odd.

Van's father would play the ball game out on the sidewalk, also. The yard might need mowing; it might be thick with weeds, and sometimes the weeds reached over Van's head, but they still played. He'd hurl the ball toward Van and he'd try to block it, the red plastic slapping his little hands. Then Van would throw it back at his knees and he'd block it. The mosquitoes and grasshoppers afflicted him. He swatted at Van's face and at times his father chucked the ball at Van's legs when he seemed distracted.

But Van learned that if he cried, he won. His mother would lift Van to her arms.

"This is too *rough*—he's just a little kid."

"We were just playing, Kell," he'd say. "He just got tired suddenly."

"He got tired because you played too rough."

Van had strong legs and he could feel himself growing. His mother fed him well and pretty soon Van would be able to run fast and jump high and throw far.

Van wanted to beat his father at the ball game. He wanted to make *him* cry in the swarm of insects. He stared at the colorful orbs above his crib. He could stand and touch them. He'd whack the orbs and watch them spin. Around and around and around, like the planets, like the galaxies, like the universe.

1

In the crib nothing mattered. In the crib everyone and everything was at peace. In the crib he could hear the hum of the stars. In the crib the world rotated above him. In the crib food was free and milk available at every utterance. In the crib there was no need for talking. In the crib talking could be attempted. In the crib he could be naked or clothed and nobody cared. In the crib he could watch animals crouch and race across the floor in desperation. In the crib he could smell the pungency of earth. In the crib he could taste meat with his nose. In the crib he could hear the squirrels in the attic, the mice in the walls, smell the cigarette fumes emanate from below. In the crib there was light, there was darkness, and everything in between. In the crib the sunlight slanted through open curtains until she came to close them. In the crib he received her ministrations. In the crib he felt eyes upon him from the hallway. In the crib he smelled the smell of men, and heard laughter. In the crib he saw shadows in the corners. In the crib he didn't need to think or feel or try to do. In the crib he could rise to the occasion, as he saw fit. In the crib he could feel those calloused hands upon him. In the crib he could feel his clothes removed and his hands placed inside others. In the crib he could cry, but he didn't want to. In the crib he could huddle and this is what he did.

0

It wasn't *him*. It was *another* him.

We are united, he thought, the roundness and the flagellating tail. We are protected, though the others passed through us with their tails and tried to penetrate.

Nothing can separate us now.

No, it wasn't his. It was another's. The dullness in his eyes. The distance, the way he seemed like an older, caring friend. It's not the same.

This one was different.

A fire in the belly.

I would give everything to know for sure who it was, Van thought. This one was separate. She would know this all along. She would play along, a majestic charade. He sensed these things.

All those years.

It was unspoken, as so much is. We are our own diviners.

Van had to be.

How different it would be if it was him. Everything divined.

We are united. We are ready to grow.

It all awaits us.

Nathan Leslie won the 2019 Washington Writers' Publishing House prize for fiction for his book *Hurry Up and Relax*. Nathan is the author of thirteen previous books including *Three Men*, *Root and Shoot*, *Sibs*, and *The Tall Tale of Tommy Twice*. He is also the author of a collection of poems, *Night Sweat*. His fiction has been published in hundreds of literary magazines such as *Shenandoah*, *North American Review*, *Boulevard*, *South Dakota Review*, *Hotel Amerika*, and *Cimarron Review*. Nathan's nonfiction has been published in *The Washington Post*, *Kansas City Star*, and *Orlando Sentinel*, among others. Nathan holds an MFA from the University of Maryland and has taught creative writing at Northern Virginia Community College for over twenty years.